Halloween Land

by

Kevin J. Kennedy

Halloween Land

Halloween Land © 2021 Kevin J. Kennedy

Cover design by François Vaillancourt

Edited by Natasha Sinclair

Artwork by Mar Garcia

All rights reserved. No part of this publication may be reproduced, distributed, or transmitted in any form or by any means, including photocopying, recording, or other electronic or mechanical methods, without the prior written permission of the publisher, except in the case of brief quotations embodied in critical reviews and certain other non-commercial uses permitted by copyright law.

First Printing, 2021

Kevin J. Kennedy

Other Books by KJK Publishing

Anthologies

Collected Christmas Horror Shorts

Collected Easter Horror Shorts

Collected Halloween Horror Shorts

Collected Christmas Horror Shorts 2

The Horror Collection: Gold Edition

The Horror Collection: Black Edition

The Horror Collection: Purple Edition

The Horror Collection: White Edition

The Horror Collection: Silver Edition

The Horror Collection: Emerald Edition

The Horror Collection: Pink Edition

The Horror Collection: Pumpkin Edition

The Horror Collection: Yellow Edition

100 Word Horrors

100 Word Horrors: Part 2

100 Word Horrors: Book 3

100 Word Horrors: Book 4

Halloween Land

Carnival of Horror

The Best of Indie Horror

Novels & Novellas

Pandemonium by J.C. Michael

You Only Get One Shot by Kevin J. Kennedy & J.C. Michael

Screechers by Kevin J. Kennedy & Christina Bergling

Stitches by Steven Stacy & Kevin J. Kennedy

Collections

Dark Thoughts by Kevin J. Kennedy

Vampiro and Other Strange Tales of the Macabre by Kevin J. Kennedy

Merry Fuckin' Christmas and other Yuletide Shit by Kevin J. Kennedy

Kevin J. Kennedy

This book is dedicated to my mum, my dad, my wife, my daughter and my three little cats.

Foreword

Desperation had brought me into the characterless building, nestled by an old cigarette factory, the great Glasgow Royal Infirmary and the Necropolis; the east end's death-row. Here, the seedy hands of ruthless business greedily tore clothes from the backs of the poor or 'sub-prime' markets as they'd call it, an attempt to legitimise their immoral basis for the establishment.

It was circa 2006, and in this place where education, morality and humanity go to ruin, I found myself surrounded by zombies and sleazy chancers — salesmen. Where punters and workers were as desperate as one another. This is where I met Kennedy.

I know what you're thinking, and no, it wasn't a strip club (not this time) — that would be moralistically far less sleazy and less dicey. No, I met Kennedy where many decent folks find themselves, often through no fault of their own — a call centre, one of the circles of Hell.

In this disconnected number-driven sea of desperate dials and yammering voices, we swam in the festering sewage of this 'work'. Kennedy has the gift of the gab, a characteristic I've long admired. He's an unexpected, explosive little package, and meeting in this environment — my first call centre, he was a cool breeze in the stagnant cesspit. We quickly established some shared mutual associations and a literary connection — specifically an insatiable appetite for horror. It's much like with alternative music fans; you spy a metal shirt in a crowded room, hear a recognisable riff or growl leak from an earbud, and you just know there's a kindred spirit in the midst. In this case, it was a book. Yes, horror breeds the same camaraderie in fans as alternative music.

Halloween Land

We became drinking buddies, even sampled a horror reading/writing group in the city. Being an introvert myself, the group chat disparaged me from returning — too much chatter, too little action! So, back to the drink it was, exchanging tales and thoughts, sharing the odd rant. The corner of Hell in which we met soon liquidised and the kamikaze of youth's '20's sent us once again on separate paths.

Until our paths collided when I picked up one of Kennedy's books, and we ended up sharing space in several anthologies throughout the fateful year of 2020. Who knew that jumping from that dreary call centre in 2006 to 14 years later, we would once again be crossing paths, this time in the glorious world of writing and publishing indie horror. After inviting me to submit a story to KJK Publishing's The Horror Collection series, a new working relationship organically formed. I am honoured that Kennedy has entrusted me with editing and supporting the continued production of The Horror Collection and his debut solo novella, which you are about to delve into; Halloween Land.

Halloween Land is a comfort-food horror tale. It's a story that would be a great introduction to this rich and diverse genre for young adults or a nostalgic horror getaway for aficionados. It's a light read, but it is rich, fun and creative. Halloween Land is a coming-of-age adventure horror that nods to classics many will recognise. It's fresh and comfortingly familiar. One of my favourite things about Halloween Land is the exploration of human connection through the two youths, Wendy and Zak. How our expectations of how life will pan out and who will be in it are, more often than not, not to be. But, if we just take a breather from our own idea of how things 'should' or 'could' be, we open up to boundless possibilities. And the relationships we thought we'd have can be far richer through empathy, support, understanding and shared growth. Even when that growth requires space. Sometimes we need our friends (including those found within the pages of our most treasured books) to help each other become better versions of ourselves, like Wendy and Zak and the global indie horror movement.

It's my honour to take your ticket and open the gates — welcome to Kevin J. Kennedy's Halloween Land!

— Natasha Sinclair 09/03/2021

(Author & Editor, ClanWitch.com)

Kevin J. Kennedy

Praise for the book:

"A fun, spook-filled throwback that evokes Laymon and R. L. Stein in equal measure... imbued with a real sense of adventure."
— Kyle M. Scott, author of The Club and Dark Island

"Kennedy has given us a great tale, reminiscent of Bradbury. Halloween Land was truly a joy to read." **— Andrew Lennon, author of A Life to Waste**

"Kevin J. Kennedy's Halloween Land peeled back the years of adulthood and revived the youthful lover of All Hallows' Eve inside me. This fun and frightening tale of a Halloween carnival with sinister intentions captivated and entertained me from beginning to end. Buy your ticket now... but beware of the Funhouse!"
— Ronald Kelly, author of Fear, Undertaker's Moon, and Irish Gothic

"A genuinely creepy, nostalgic romp from light into deepest darkness."
— Christopher Motz, author of Pine Lakes and A Hostile Takeover

Halloween Land

"Kennedy's 'Halloween Land' comes at you a million miles an hour. Filled with as much emotional depth as carnage. This one will have you hooked from page one!"
— Steve Stred, author of Ritual

"If the thought of crazed clowns and killer carnivals have you trembling from both fear and anticipation, then Kevin Kennedy's Halloweenland is the nightmarish novella that you need."
— J.C. Michael, author of Pandemonium and You Only Get One Shot

"Old school horror clashes with new in this surgically-lean coming of age tale. Hip, and well-seasoned with blood and carnage, just the thing to get you in the Halloween spirit."
— Tim Curran, author of Clownflesh and Bioterror

"Part Bradbury, part Laymon, Halloween Land is something straight off the paperback horror rack! Classic horror fans need to check this out."
— Glenn Rolfe, author of August's Eyes and Until Summer Comes Around

Halloween Land
by
Kevin J. Kennedy

The alarm hadn't even gone off when Zak jumped up out of bed. Not that Zak often set an alarm for Saturday mornings. However, this Saturday was different; it was only 7am when he decided to start his day. Having barely slept a wink, he knew there was no way he was getting back to sleep now the sun was finally rising. He had to get round to Wendy's as soon as possible. He knew she was as excited about tonight's events as he was and doubted that she would have slept much, either.

Wendy was Zak's best friend; they had always been friends from as far back as he could remember. Their mothers had been friends and had taken them to the same nursery, where Zak and Wendy had played together. Now, at the age of thirteen, they would often spend their time either getting into trouble or trying to get each other out of trouble. It wasn't that they were bad kids, they were just typical teenagers who had a knack for making bad decisions. They had both been on their best behaviour for the last two weeks to ensure that they didn't risk being put on house arrest by their parents. Zak and Wendy loved Halloween, and this wasn't just any old Halloween; this was the Halloween that Halloween Land was coming to town!

The flyers for Halloween Land had started appearing around town about a month before. They were crudely designed, with a picture of a funhouse that looked like it had been drawn by a child, printed in jet black ink. The flyers looked like they had been ripped into shape rather than cut with a machine or scissors, and the paper resembled the cheap paper towels that companies buy when they don't care about their employees. Zak had found his first one in Cult Empire Comics, where he was picking up the new copies of Vietnam Zombie Holocaust and City of Lost Souls. They had a pile of the flyers next to the cash register. Zak had picked it up because it looked retro — therefore cool, and thought he could add it to the assortment of random pictures, posters and art prints that adorned his walls. It hadn't given any details of what Halloween Land would be or where it was. The obvious guess was that a travelling carnival was coming to town, but it turned out to be much bigger than that.

As the weeks passed, Zak and Wendy tried their best to find any details of Halloween Land online. There wasn't a single mention of it anywhere. They had busied themselves with deciding what costumes they would wear on the night itself, regardless of where they ended up. Wendy settled on a 'Wednesday Addams' costume, and Zak opted for an 'Evil Clown' costume. Wendy tried to talk him out of it due to her phobia of clowns, but he insisted that Halloween was supposed to be scary and she would just need to deal with it. While she wasn't happy, she convinced herself she would be okay as long as she saw Zak with the mask off first.

The week before Halloween, everything was revealed. The old pier had been bought by an anonymous investor. The council put an advert in the local newspaper about how it would be refurbished and that it would create lots of jobs, not to mention additional tourism and revenue for the town. Apparently, the buyer was going to convert it back to its glory days and have it filled with various stalls and rides. As a special opening night, they were going to theme the mini-carnival as Halloween Land. The flyers became more extravagant, boasting cheesy slogans like 'If you come along, you'll never want to leave us!' and 'The most terrifying Halloween evening of your life!'. Zak couldn't wait. Part of the reason that Zak and Wendy's friendship had lasted into high school, while many others didn't make it, was in part due to their mutual love of old, cheesy horror movies. Zak's dad had a massive collection of horror movies from the eighties and nineties. Most were on DVD, but he even had an old VHS recorder set up in his study and loads of old tapes. Zak would often sneak in after his parents were in bed and watch some of his dad's old movies. The acting was terrible in some of them, and the special effects were worse, but Zak loved them, nonetheless. He had then started sneaking them out to Wendy, who would take them home for just the one night and watch them in her room, then they would swap notes the next day; that was when they were younger. Now, they just watched them together, and none of their parents seemed to pay much attention — as long as they left their bedroom door open. That was the annoying new rule; no matter whose house they were in, they had to leave the door open. It really frustrated them both that they weren't allowed privacy just because they had gotten older, but they both knew you had to pick and choose your battles with your parents. None of that mattered right now, though. Halloween Land was coming to town.

As each day passed, in the week leading up to Halloween, there were still very few details about the new carnival that would sit on the pier. Zak had expected to have spent the last week watching workmen refurbish the old pier, but nothing happened. It looked as bad as it ever had and was still a regular hang out for the local junkies. The other thing that he found very strange, but no one seemed to be talking about, was that no rides were being assembled. He started to wonder if it would be just a few small rides, and all the excitement would be for nothing.

On the thirtieth of October, Zak and Wendy walked out to where the old pier began, a place that no reputable person in town would venture any more. The drunks and the junkies had made it their own; hanging out at the end of the pier, knowing that the police would never venture down there. Only the odd couple would wander halfway on the way home from a night club for a quickie before staggering home. You can actually divide the pier up from where the pairs of discarded panties start and finish to where the broken needles start. Zak and Wendy looked along the pier as far as they could see — before their view was blocked by one of the old gift shops. It was made of wood and the weather hadn't been kind to it. The paint was cracked, and the wood seemed to sag in places. Most of the panes of glass were broken or gone completely. Zak wasn't sure how they could get the place looking semi-presentable by the next day, never mind safe for the public, but he didn't care about that. It had been advertised everywhere, for a month. He knew that there was no way that it wouldn't happen. It was only one more day. He would enjoy himself, even if it was a run-down dump.

***

Zak's brain was buzzing as he rang Wendy's doorbell. There had been an advert on the radio about Halloween Land just before he left the house. Apparently, someone had been there first thing in the morning and raved about how amazing it all looked. Zak found it a little hard to believe, considering the state the pier had been in only the day before, but the reporter or radio DJ sounded convincing in what he was saying.

"Oh, hi, Zak. Come on in," Wendy's mum said, as she waved Zak inside. "Wendy will be down just now."

Zak walked straight through to the kitchen, as was his Saturday morning routine at Wendy's. What wasn't normal was when Wendy appeared in the kitchen, already dressed in her 'Wednesday Addams' costume.

"Uh, isn't it a little early for costumes?"

"It's Halloween, isn't it, dummy?" Wendy responded, rolling her eyes and glancing away.

Halloween Land

She really does look like Wednesday Addams, Zak thought.

"Well, yeh, but it's daytime…" Zak responded, wondering if he was arguing a point or looking for a good enough reason to go put his own costume on.

"Look, we have a big day ahead of us, and I just didn't want to have to come home later to get changed. This way, I'm ready for whatever comes up, and I don't need to be home 'til eleven tonight. My mum said since she knows I love Halloween, and because she knows the entire town will be there, I can have an extra hour. She said everyone in her work has been talking about tonight and that she doesn't know anyone who isn't going…" Wendy paused for a moment, slipping into one of her trance-like states before she snapped back into reality and continued on an excited rant. "You know, we are going to have to queue for ages to get on anything. I think we need to be there early because people will probably queue, but if we get in first, we should be able to have a go on a good few rides before the pier fills up." As Wendy finished her excited chatter, Zak was still wondering if he should go put his own costume on.

"Uh, yeah, whatever you say. Do you think I should, maybe, go get my costume just now?" Zak asked, not really having listened to what Wendy said.

"Might as well. Will save us having to stop whatever we are doing later." As the words came out of Wendy's mouth, she felt a sense of dread, unconsciously sealing her own fate. Now she would have to spend the day with psycho-clown-guy. Maybe it wouldn't be so bad. At least she was getting to spend the full day with Zak.

"Okay, let's go back to mine, so I can get ready," Zak said excitedly.

A Few Hours Later...

When Zak and Wendy arrived at the pier, they couldn't believe the transformation. Not only was the entire pier filled with stalls and rides, but they had even converted some of the old shops, and everything looked like new. Neither of them could understand how the carnies had managed to do so much in so little time, but they didn't really care. They were amongst the first to arrive; after they each bought a large reel of tickets, they darted eagerly through the newly built carnival gates.

Kevin J. Kennedy

At first, they hadn't had to queue to get onto the rides, but the carnival had quickly come to life. People of all ages descended on the pier — the flashing illuminations of vivid colour drew them in. Calliope music played from each individual vendor, the tunes blending together in a happy melody. Bells and horns went off as the townsfolk won prizes at the stalls testing skill or strength. Almost everyone knew that these games were rigged — it was rarely skill that made you a winner, but people played them for fun and reminiscence of simpler times. All of the stalls and rides were painted with witches with black cats, jack-o-lanterns, vampires and the like. Some of them even had fake ghosts hanging with light-up eyes, and most of them had smoke machines hooked up, giving the flooring of the pier a layer of mystical-like mist. Wendy just hoped they had gotten rid of all the needles that the junkies used to shoot up, though she was pretty sure they would have, considering the job they had done on the place.

As night fell, Zak and Wendy made their way between the revellers, enjoying the various sweet smells that enveloped the air. There were candy apples, candy floss, roasted peanuts, freshly made doughnuts, crepes, chocolate-coated bananas, burgers, hotdogs, and much more. Just about any kind of food that was bad for you but tasted great was at the carnival. Zak and Wendy had grabbed a burger and chilli-cheese fries when they arrived but had decided to leave some of the messier snacks 'til the end of the night.

Wendy found that the scary clown costume that Zak had worn wasn't giving her the creeps. It helped knowing it was her best friend inside it; she knew him well enough that no matter how he was dressed, she recognised his movements and actions. On top of that, he had to keep lifting his mask to eat or when he got too hot. When they were walking down to the pier, they agreed that they would leave the funhouse until after it got dark. They were now making their way to the end of the pier where the newly built funhouse now stood. Moving through the dense crowd was slow now, though neither of them were in a rush.

Now that night had fallen, it felt like an entirely different carnival. Darkness lends a feeling of magic to carnivals; the flashing, coloured lights coupled with the enchanting music had them feeling like they were part of another world. Another world of whimsy, magic and excitement — where anything could happen — even if only for one night. As the crowd thickened towards the end of the pier, the two huddled tighter together. Wendy took the opportunity to slip her arm through Zak's. It was something that she had never done before, but she felt this was the perfect opportunity. Zak turned towards her, looked down at their interlinked arms and back up to her face. Wendy could see his cheeks redden, even in the dark, as his mask rested across his forehead.

They had never been more than friends, but recently Zak had started to look at her differently. Wendy had noticed straight away, and after some careful thought, she had decided that it wouldn't be so bad if he was to ask to be her boyfriend. Zak was pretty shy, so Wendy decided a few days before the carnival that it would be the perfect time to try and subtly show him that she liked him more than just a friend. She knew he had always had a crush on the Wednesday Addams character, hence the costume choice.

As they walked between the stalls and rides, occasionally stopping to walk around the newly set-up mini arcades, they both noticed that some of the carnies were pretty weird. They had both seen a fair number of movies containing carnival freaks but hadn't expected to come across any in real life. Neither of them had seen any actual freaks yet, and the carnies operating the rides and stalls all seemed pretty normal, but every so often they would see someone who looked a little off.

The freaks crept around in the background, not necessarily hiding but definitely staying out of the way. Zak and Wendy wondered if they were simply people in costume, hired to make the place look a little scarier, but if that was so, the 'costumes' were pretty high end — it would've been a waste to not show them off. One of the freaks had four arms and appeared to be using all of them. It seemed elaborate for someone that a lot of the revellers would only get a passing glance at. There was a woman who crawled on all fours, but her arms and legs looked disproportionately long, and the bends at the elbows and knees didn't look right either. It was as if she was a giant pink spider that was missing a few limbs. They saw a man that must have been eight-foot tall, but he too stayed skulking in the shadows. It was a little scary, but they both guessed that would be the point of a carnival-themed on Halloween. It just seemed like it would have made more sense to have them walking around the pier and scaring people, but maybe their costumes weren't as effective close up; perhaps they were better off in the dark.

They passed a Gypsy caravan with a strange little dwarf standing outside. He was barely three-foot tall and looked grumpy. His skin was old and looked weather-beaten.

"He looks like a hardened version of Hoggle from the Labyrinth," Zak said.

Wendy snickered, thinking he had said it too loud. She knew what he meant, but the dwarf was much more serious and looked better built.

He was calling out for people to come inside and have their fortune told by Madame de Rosemonde. Wendy thought about it for a little while before deciding that it was better not knowing. Something about the caravan and the strange little dwarf just didn't feel right. She couldn't work out what it was, but she had a feeling inside that the fortune teller was real, unlike most; she felt like the fortune teller was already probing inside her head through the caravan walls. Wendy wasn't sure if she wanted to know her future. Zak noticed her hesitation; her body language undeniably changed — Wendy's interlocked arm tensed as though she was pulling towards the caravan.

"Wanna go in?" he asked.

"No, I was just looking," she responded, before pulling him forward.

As they walked away, Madame de Rosemonde exited her caravan and stood next to the dwarf, named Doc. She had long red hair, her face was powdered white, and her lips were dark red. She was extremely attractive. Dressed in typical Romany Gypsy clothing, with layers of patterned floaty scarves and beads. She leant against the side of the caravan and watched the two kids disappear into the crowd.

"Good kids, those two," she said to Doc as she disappeared back into her caravan with a sombre look on her face.

Zak and Wendy were now struggling to push through the crowd. The bottom of the pier was heaving. A lot of people seemed to be heading towards the funhouse. When they finally arrived at the queue, they sighed in unison. There had to be a hundred people, and the strange-looking clown at the entrance seemed to be only letting groups of two or three in at a time.

The queue didn't seem to be getting shorter when Wendy had a lightbulb moment that she hoped would make time go by a little quicker.

"I'm pretty cold. Do you think you could wrap your arms around me while we wait?" she asked, looking up at Zak, who was slightly taller than her, with her doe-like eyes. Zak, a little taken aback by the request, kept his composure and nodded. He had wanted to hold Wendy in his arms for a while now but didn't know if she liked him back. As he stepped behind her and wrapped his arms around her, his mind went into overdrive. *Does this mean she likes me? She took my arm earlier. Or is she just cold, and didn't want us to get separated earlier?*

As Zak's mind raced, Wendy just enjoyed the feeling of being so close to him. She didn't know if they would have their first kiss that night, but she knew that it was definitely the beginning of something. Her heart pounding in her chest was enough to reassure her of that.

Before they knew it, they were at the front of the queue, and they had barely spoken the whole time, both caught up in their thoughts of the future together without either being able to vocalise their feelings.

One of the most beautiful clowns that either of them had ever seen was stood at the funhouse entrance. Her make-up was white and black. It surrounded her eyes and mouth, her eyes darkened along the lids, and a sharp line ran through both eyes from the brow to the cheek. Surrounding her pink, luscious lips was a thick, white rim that came to points at either side of her face, outlined in a thin, black line. The rest of her face had no paint on it. Her outfit seemed a little weird for a clown; she wore black and red pop socks, bare legs with little wine-coloured shorts with white lace around the leg holes. Her top was a black vest with a large blue silky bow around her neck. Her puffed-out, long, ginger hair was topped off with a gold top hat with a blue and wine oversized bow wrapped around it. She wore white lace cuffs on both wrists.

"Tickets?" the clown asked them. Neither of them had ever seen a clown look so sad. It wasn't the clown make-up that made her look sad. She just looked like she would rather be anywhere else than standing taking tickets for the funhouse. Zak stuck his hand out, holding two tickets. They had been paying each other onto rides since the start of the night, taking turns each. The clown just nodded her head to the side, towards the entrance.

The entrance to the funhouse was a massive goblin face, bright green and split down the middle. Zak and Wendy walked towards it, and Zak pushed the doors open. Ahead of them stood a long, dark corridor. With a last look at each other, they both stepped inside, the doors swung shut behind them. As soon as the doors closed, all noise from outside ceased. The chattering of the crowd, the calliope music and the various bells and buzzers that had been ringing were all gone. The corridor had no lights, but there were tiny, little, white cat eyes along the floor so they could see the walkway. They made their way along the corridor to the first turn. As they turned the corner, an almighty roar ripped through the corridor — a man-sized corpse now blocked their path. Neither of them screamed. The metal pole that was attached to its head swung it out from the wall. It wasn't concealed nearly enough, not to mention that the corpse had a distinct plastic look to it. The rest of the funhouse wasn't much better. By the time they were walking down a corridor to the exit, both were feeling deeply let down by the claims the flyers had made.

Halloween Land

As Zak pushed the doors open to the outside world, they both noticed a few things straight away. The noises that had been there before didn't return. Where earlier there had been hundreds, if not thousands of people talking to each other at once with music playing from everywhere, there was now only a few separate calliope tunes playing from various points on the pier. They sounded distant and eerie on their own, the sound of the ocean hitting the legs of the pier and the beach almost drowning them out. It made them sound like a broken jack in the box. It was now fully dark, and most of the rides had been turned off, but more disturbing was the lack of anyone else on the pier. Nervously they both stepped out onto the walkway of the funhouse that led to the stairs to leave.

"So, you made it through?" the beautiful, sad clown asked them.

"What? Where is everyone?" Zak asked, turning to her with a quizzical look on his face. "How long were we in there?"

For the first time, the kids saw the clown smile.

"You were in about fifteen minutes, and technically everyone is still here. Well, most of them anyway."

"What do you mean everyone is still here?" Wendy asked, looking across the pier, trying to convince herself that she wasn't missing something.

"Well, the funhouse is a kind of magic portal. It feeds the carnival. Some who pass through come out of the exit, just like you two did, and others, the carnival decides to keep for itself. That's the magic of the carnival or the best way I can explain it anyway. I'm not sure I fully understand it all myself," the clown responded, still looking glum.

Wendy and Zak looked at each other for a second before looking back at the clown.

"You're fucking with us. It's some kind of trick, isn't it?" Zak said, with a pleading look in his eyes. He knew something was wrong, but he was unable to believe what the clown was saying.

"Nope," the clown answered. "I've only been with the carnival for a little while, but it would seem that it's powered by souls. Nothing to do with me though, I just work here," she concluded.

"What, so you're telling me everyone else has been swallowed up by some crazy funhouse at a stupid carnival? Bullshit!" Zak exclaimed — in a voice that was much less forceful than he planned it to be. Wendy was now holding his arm again, and pressed tight against his side.

The clown sighed. "Listen, I don't really give a fuck what you believe or don't believe. It is what it is, just like most things in life. Not believing it doesn't mean you don't have to deal with it." The clown stopped talking and appraised the two teenagers. "Okay, this is how it works, as best as I've come to understand it. The carnival travels from place to place, never appearing for more than a day. The next day it's gone, as are all traces of it. Each time it leaves a town, it takes a few of the residents with it. It always has, and it always will."

"So, where is everyone else then if it only takes a few people? And what does the funhouse have to do with it all?" Zak asked. Unsure as to whether he believed what she was saying, his only option was to question her more.

Halloween Land

"The funhouse is kind of the centre of the carnival, the power source or the heart if you like. The carnival doesn't just travel from town to town, it crosses planes of existence and sometimes even time-hops. Today we are here, but tomorrow we could be in the old west, and the following day we could be back here again, on the very same day but in an alternate reality that is only slightly different from this one. The carnival morphs into whatever fits the surroundings and time period. Sometimes it's a massive theme park, and other times it's a tiny travelling sideshow. As I said, I haven't been here that long, but I've seen some pretty interesting things," the clown explained.

"This has to be some kind of joke. Did someone put you up to this? Someone from school?"

"Kid, look around you. Do you really think this is a joke? Everyone else is here. You two are here too, but also not here," the clown said, looking around her. "You're here until the carnival decides if it's going to let you leave."

"But I thought you said the funhouse decides? Aren't we free to go?"

"The funhouse has decided you are free to go, but there are a lot of crazies this side of the veil. You still need to make it back to a safe piece of land. If either of you make it to the end of the pier, you will be safe. As soon as your feet hit concrete, you can go home and go about your life as it was before. Tomorrow a few people will be missing, but that's nothing out of the ordinary. The carnival, and all traces of it, will be gone forever, and no one will even remember it was here. I wish you good luck on your journey, my friends. Watch out for those carnies." With that, the clown jumped straight up, with her arms extended, catching onto the balcony above. She was up and over the balcony with incredible acrobatic speed and ease, leaving them standing alone.

"This can't be real, can it?" Wendy asked, looking at Zak with eyes filled with fear.

"I don't know. I mean, how would you fake this? Where the fuck is everyone? They couldn't have emptied the pier that quickly. Let's just head home. I don't think any good can come from hanging about here." They quickly descended the stairs, heading straight for the entrance to the pier. It looked much creepier with most of the lights off. The few individual tunes that were still playing drifted eerily on the sea breeze, the delicious smells of the assorted foods from earlier now gone, replaced by the smell of salt water and seaweed. Wendy slipped her hand down from their interlocking arms and clasped her fingers through Zak's.

"Let's get out of here," she said, picking up her pace.

They started to move quickly through the now creepy-looking stalls, steeped in shadows, making the carnival appear as if it had been abandoned for years. Suddenly three shapes stepped out in front of them. Wendy let out a gasp, and they both stopped in their tracks. In front of them stood three clowns, Wendy's worst nightmare. More terrifying for her was that each of these clowns had a carved pumpkin for a face — not make-up to look like a pumpkin — but what actually seemed to be a moving, living, (possibly breathing) pumpkin face. Their mouths were carved exactly as they would be on a pumpkin carved for Halloween, except Wendy and Zak could tell that their teeth were razor sharp. Zak grabbed Wendy's hand and started running, pulling her with him. They ducked between stalls and rides, moving as fast as they could while trying not to trip on all the electrical cables that were running along the ground. As they moved, they could hear a strained, guttural laughing that sounded like it was coming from the roofs of the stalls above and behind them. As the kids came out between one of the burger bars and a novelty shop, they were both panting hard. Knowing they couldn't keep running, Wendy looked around for somewhere to hide.

"Look, over there," she said to Zak, pointing.

Zak smiled, and they took off running together, straight for the shooting gallery. Both vaulted the counter and landed safely behind it. Zak quickly pulled two of the guns down from the rack. When they had played the game earlier, they were both impressed with the force in which the ball-bearings fired out of the rifles. What they didn't know is if they would have any effect at all on the clowns.

"Stay down," Zak protectively told Wendy. "I'll look and see if they've followed us."

As Zak began to peek over the counter he instantly felt something smash into his forehead, knocking him flying back on his ass. Wendy screamed again and crawled quickly towards him. Zak raised his hand to his forehead. "What the fuck was that?" Wendy touched her hand to his forehead. He winced. Bringing her fingers up to her nose and sniffing, she said, "It's pumpkin. They are throwing pumpkins at us."

"Are you fucking kidding me? We are running from these clowns, and they are throwing pumpkins?" Zak said as the pumpkin-clowns seemed to laugh at him in their strange guttural way.

Wendy was shocked at the look of rage that crossed Zak's face; she had never seen him get angry before.

"Think this is all a big fucking joke, do they?" he mumbled as he crawled across the ground and retrieved his gun. This time he crawled over to the stall wall and slid up behind the side of the window. "Wendy, throw one of those stupid teddies out the window and over to the side."

There were large plastic bags of teddies under the table she was lying next to. Ripping open the first bag, she grabbed one of the smaller teddies and crawled below the window to the stall. She looked towards Zak, who nodded. He had gotten a glimpse of the three clowns standing out in the open for a millisecond before the pumpkin had almost knocked his head off. *Just like a coconut shy,* he thought to himself. Wendy threw the teddy as hard as she could without looking over the counter. As it left her hand, Zak spun around the side of the window, raising his gun as he turned, took aim and pulled the trigger. The clown in the middle's head exploded upon impact; sections of pumpkin flew everywhere, but there was more. The pumpkin seemed to have some form of skull inside, and shards flew into the air, some stabbing into the pier's wooden floor and others sticking into the sides of stalls. The red and orange mess covering the two clowns next to the middle one was a mix of blood and pumpkin guts. It was red and orange and had partially congealed lumps that dripped from the other clowns. Zak had no idea if it would even have any effect on the clowns, but it seemed that their heads weren't all that tough.

Halloween Land

The clowns on either side of the middle one turned from the flying teddy hurtling towards their headless colleague. Zak took the chance to aim again and shot the second clown in the head. His aim was as true as the first shot. As the second clown's head exploded, the first clown's lifeless body fell to the ground. The third clown ran straight towards the shooting gallery. Zak hadn't expected it and fired a shot that went wild. As he readjusted his aim and pulled the trigger again, the gun clicked, but nothing came out. Zak tried again just as the clown dove through the stall window and landed at Wendy's feet.

Wendy screamed, fell backwards and tried to crawl away, but the clown grabbed her by the ankle. Wendy, never one to just lay down, started kicking the clown in the face with her free foot, but Zak could see she that had to time it to miss the razor-sharp teeth of the animated pumpkin head.

Zak tried to get another shot off. He was at point-blank range, but the gun just wouldn't fire. Having no time left, Zak spun the gun so that he held it by the barrel and swung it with all his might at the clown's head. The stock had an equally pleasing effect on the pumpkin-clown's head as the ball-bearings did. While the head didn't quite explode apart as it had before, it'd burst in several places; chunks of the innards spilled out, spraying Wendy's legs with the red and orange bloody gunge before the clown collapsed on top of her. Zak wasted no time checking that the outside of the stall was clear, before grabbing the clown by the back of its suit and dragging it from Wendy. He grabbed her hands and pulled her to a standing position.

"Euuchhhh!" Wendy said as she wiped the mushed pumpkin from her legs. It looked different from normal pumpkin innards — redder as if it had blood running through it.

"Are you okay?" Zak worried.

"Yeh, I'm fine. It didn't bite me. And thanks."

"Let's get the fuck out of here before any more of those things appear."

As if tempting fate, as the kids vaulted the window of the shooting gallery, they noticed more of the clowns appearing on the roofs of several stalls. Each wore a different style of clown suit, but they all had the same large pumpkin head. They had no eyes but a strange light inside the sockets that looked, most peculiarly, like a candle flickering. Each of them started to make strange gargled sounds. Zak and Wendy had no idea if they were communicating or if this was the collective sound of their hunger. Not waiting to find out, Zak grabbed her hand and started running. In his rush, he had forgotten to lift the gun. It wasn't firing, but he could have used it as a club. Wendy however, had lifted the gun she had left lying next to the bag of teddies.

They sprinted down the centre of the pier, no longer concerned with trying to hide but instead going for the most direct route out of the carnival. As they ran, Zak felt something lightly hit the back of his head before falling around his neck. His hands went up quickly to wrap around the yellow rubber ring that now hung around his neck. Slowing to a walking pace, with Wendy stopping to look at Zak to see what was going on, another hoop, green this time, came flying out of the darkness and landed perfectly around Wendy's neck.

"Are they actually playing ring-toss with us?" Wendy said, sounding both shocked and angry.

"Looks like it. Let's keep going. We're almost there."

As they started to run again, the rings began landing all around them and bouncing away. The clowns strange chatter was getting louder as they neared the entrance to the pier. The kids soon noticed that the rings landing around them were on fire. All it would take was for one to find its mark, and one of them were in for some serious burns.

"Keep going," Zak said, struggling to catch his breath. They passed the last of the stalls and rides, entering the large open part of the pier just before the gate — they stopped in their tracks. In front of them stood three of the strangest looking creatures they had ever seen. They looked like a hideous blend of an overly-muscular Rottweiler, with the head of a wolf, only the head and snout of the wolf-shaped face was also made out of pumpkin. Bright orange, just like the clowns' faces, except the dog-like creature's jaws snapped much faster and had a lot more teeth. The beast's bodies were covered in jet-black fur — as if it belonged to a normal dog.

Not knowing quite what to do, and knowing they only had one gun, Zak turned to look behind them. The clowns who had been lining the rooftops had now formed a line across the middle of the walkway. There were twelve of them in total, and each was doing something somewhere between weird and terrifying. One of the pumpkin clowns juggled three mini-pumpkins that were all on fire, another was doing a pretty impressive nunchuck display, the nunchucks also on fire. One was walking towards them on his hands with both feet on fire. The fire seemed to cause the pumpkin-clowns no pain, but Zak and Wendy doubted it would be as painless should it touch them.

Zak turned back and forth quickly between the clowns and the dog-creatures, trying to work out which route was less likely to result in a painful death. As his mind ran a million miles a minute, he heard the gun go off next to him. Wendy had taken a shot at one of the dog-creatures while he was trying to work out what to do; she never had the patience for ditherers. None of the dogs dropped.

"You missed it," Zak said.

"I hit it, they just don't go down as easy as the clowns," as Wendy finished speaking, she took another shot. This time Zak could see this one hit the dog-creature by the way its skull bounced back. It still didn't drop.

"Fuck!" Zak said, knowing they were in trouble. "Shoot the clowns. Maybe we can go back that way. Wendy spun round quickly and took aim, and fired into the approaching wall of clowns. Two of them dropped at the one time, both on separate ends of the line. The first fell off his unicycle, crashing into the pier boards, and the other just stood headless for a few seconds before crashing forwards onto the chainsaw he carried. It took only seconds for the chainsaw to rip him apart.

"What the..." Zak started as Wendy aimed again. She fired into the face of the one with the biggest pumpkin head, hoping he was some kind of leader and that his death would somehow render the others immobile. It did no such thing, but again, two more clowns went down. Zak looked back to see that the dog-creatures were making their way towards them slowly, but he had no idea when they would break into a run. As he turned back towards the clowns, Wendy was setting herself up for another shot — he caught a glimpse of gold on one of the rooftops. On peering closer, he could see it was the clown from earlier at the funhouse. He could barely make her out, but there was no hiding her ginger hair and hat. He could see the barrel of a rifle peeking out from the darkness. As he turned back towards the clowns, two more fell to the ground.

Only six remained, but the dogs were now almost upon them. Zak ran to the closest stall and jumped inside. It turned out to be the hook-a-duck stall. It was filled with plastic ducks floating in a spinning pool of water. There was pretty much nothing else in the stall, apart from the teddies for prizes and the long wooden pole with a hooked end. Zak grabbed the pole and jumped back through the stall window. When he got back outside, he could see the clown that appeared to be helping them had dropped down from the rooftop and was moving towards the pumpkin-clowns. Wendy seemed to be messing with the gun — it had either stuck, or she had run out of ball-bearings.

"Use it as a club," Zak shouted as he moved towards the dog-creatures. Two of them turned to Zak, while the other kept progressing towards Wendy.

"Behind you!" Zak shouted.

Wendy spun around and turned the gun over to use as a club. The pretty clown seemed to be doing fine on her own anyway. Zak struggled to take his eyes away from Wendy when the first dog got close enough for him to take a swing. The pole he had was long and not the easiest to handle, but he only barely missed the creature's skull. As it made a strangled, growling sound at him, red mushy chunks dropped from its maw. The other dog-creature, seeing its chance, sprung at him. Swinging his stick quickly, he hit the creature in the ribs. As it landed, he realised the hook had stuck in its ribs. Thinking quickly, he started to pull the dog backwards towards the stall he had come from. When they got in line with it, using every bit of might he could muster, Zak swung his weight into pulling the stick as quickly as possible towards the hook-a-duck stall, dragging the creature with it and smashing it against the wall. It let out a not-quite-howl and fell to its side. The force of the creature smashing into the stall had released the hook from its side. It took Zak three goes, missing with the first two, but the third time he crashed the pole down, the hook solidly sunk into the creature's pumpkin-like skull.

Wasting no time, Zak spun to see the other two dog-creatures were closing in on Wendy. One at either side of her. The hook of his pole would not come free from the dead creature's skull, and he had no time to find another weapon. Wendy was swinging furiously at the dog-creature closest to her, which seemed to be keeping it at bay, but she allowed the other to get closer to her. Without a second thought, Zak charged the dog closest to him and took the hardest penalty kick he had ever swung. The front of his foot crashed into the creature's ribcage, and he felt the bones snap as it let out a blood-curdling howl, the sound still gargled by whatever made up its vocal cords. It quickly turned to snap at him with its large, orange canines, its last-ditch attempt, as it was obvious that it was hurt. Taking his time to aim his next kick, Zak danced on the spot. The creature attacked again; Zak waited until it just missed him and swung another full-force kick, this time aiming for the creature's jaw. When his foot connected, the jaw snapped shut. As its teeth smashed together, part of the jaw broke off, landing between its two front paws. As Zak looked on, wondering what his next move was, Wendy came from nowhere, the gun held over her head and brought it down on the creature's skull. The first strike killed it instantly, but Zak watched as she continued to rain down blows. When she finally stopped, the corpse was almost unrecognisable. Zak looked to where she had been and found the other animal lying dead, in a similar state. Remembering the pumpkin-dogs hadn't been their only concern, he turned back to where that battle of the clowns had been going on. They were all dead, their bodies strewn all over the pier. He caught sight of the pretty clown, slipping between two of the stalls.

"Wait!" Zak shouted, before jogging to catch her. As he reached the alley between the two stalls, he could see that she was gone, and he had no intentions of chasing her down the pier. Turning to go back for Wendy and get the hell out of there, he noticed a white, rectangular card lying on the pier boards. He reached down and picked it up and was shocked to see what was on it. The card had a sketch of both him and Wendy, and under the drawings were scribbled the words 'Look after these two. They're important.' On the back of the card was a printed signature of Madame de Rosemonde. Zak had no idea what it meant or why they were important, but he didn't really care. It was time to leave this place. He slipped the card into the single tiny, excuse-for-a-pocket on his costume and ran back to get Wendy. She was still standing with the club raised, looking hyper-vigilant. She visibly relaxed at the sight of Zak getting closer.

"Let's get the fuck out of here," Wendy said, as she grabbed his hand, and they ran to the edge of the pier. As soon as their feet hit the concrete at the edge of the pier, everything went hazy for the briefest flash and then they were surrounded by hundreds, if not thousands of the townspeople. They all looked in shock, some of them were injured, but it didn't look like many people could have been trapped on the pier. Zak and Wendy knew that by tomorrow reports would start to come in for missing people. Had everyone had the same experience or had it been different for each of them? Did the others receive help from some of the carnival folk, or had it just been Wendy and Zak? Each of them had a million questions, but they weren't sure anyone would have any answers.

"Let's go to my house," Wendy said. "Hopefully, my parents have made it home okay, and you can call yours."

"Didn't think I'd let you walk home yourself, did you?" Zak said, with the best smile he could muster under the circumstances. Zak wrapped his arm around Wendy's waist, pulling her in tight against him to keep her warm. His early shyness and worry about getting closer to Wendy seemed like absolute madness in light of the night they had just had. As they walked through the townsfolk, who seemed to be quietly making their way away from the pier, they stopped and turned back to have one last look at the carnival. It was gone. It had been gone the minute they stepped back on the concrete. The pier looked like it always had, rundown and in need of repair.

"Was it all an illusion?" Zak said, almost to himself.

Wendy put her arm out in front of him. The teeth marks were evident, and the blood hadn't quite dried. "I don't think so."

"We need to get you to a hospital," Zak declared, sounding panicked.

"I'm fine. It barely caught me. I just hope I don't turn into a pumpkin," Wendy remarked, trying to sound like she was joking but knowing that she was a little worried about it actually happening.

The Next Morning

When Zak got to Wendy's house, her mother had let him in, as always. He expected things to be sombre, but she seemed her usual, chirpy self. When Wendy came into the kitchen, she quickly pulled him outside.

"What's going on?" Zak demanded.

"Aren't your parents the same?" she asked in return.

"What? Uh, my parents were still asleep when I left. Why is your mum acting like nothing's happened?"

When Zak had got to Wendy's the night before, her parents were already home. They were freaking out, but really happy to see the kids come in. They made Zak call his parents straight away. They had made it home safely, too, and told him to get a taxi straight home. Both sets of parents had known that neither of the kids had taken out their mobile phones that evening, as they didn't have decent pockets in their costumes to carry them, and hadn't wanted to lose them on the rides. Knowing the kids would have gone to one house or the other, the parents had gone straight home, knowing they may never find them in the crowd outside the pier. All four parents had spoken to their kids at length about what had happened to each of them before they all headed to bed for the night, exhausted.

"They don't remember it. I noticed they seemed awful happy when I got up and knew it was strange, so instead of mentioning anything, I just asked my mum if she had a good time at the carnival, and do you know what she said..." Wendy paused for a second. "She said,

'Wonderful'. Do you believe that shit? Wonderful!" Wendy exclaimed, exasperated. "I was kinda worried that you would show up and not remember."

"How could I forget?" Zak responded.

"Everyone else seems to have forgotten what happened. I checked online— no mention of anything. I can't even find mention of the carnival anywhere or a developer buying the pier. It's all gone."

"Fuck! What do we do?" Zak asked.

"What can we do? We're safe now, and as far as I can tell, we just act as if nothing happened."

"Let's go to my house," Zak said.

At Zak's House

"It was definitely here. I'm sure I pinned it on the board," Zak said, rummaging around behind his chest of drawers to see if it had fallen. "I know I kept that fucking flyer."

"It's gone, Zak, just like everything else. That carnival...it wasn't normal. It had some kind of magic running through it. How else would you explain a fucking living pumpkin of any type?"

"Shit! One minute," Zak grabbed the clown trousers from the night before. He reached into the little mersh-lined slit of a pocket, and he felt it straight away, the card he had found after the battle.

'Look after these two. They're important.' was all it said.

They looked at each other. All traces of the carnival seemed to have disappeared apart from the card. What did it mean? Were they going to meet the strange, pretty, clown woman again? Was it Madame de Rosemonde that would cross their paths in the future? Or was it just a coincidence that the card was still there? Neither of them was in a rush to find out.

"So, what do we do? Just act like nothing happened?" Zak asked.

"Well... We could always get cosy and watch one of your dad's old horror movies," Wendy said with a little blush.

"You want to watch horror? After what we have just been through?" Zak asked, a little taken aback.

"Is there any other type of movie worth watching?" she said with a chuckle. "Besides, you can keep me close and protect me, but just to be safe, let's watch something old and cheesy."

As the kids made their way towards Zak's dad's study, they both knew that their lives had changed forever. As Wendy slipped her hand into Zak's and he clasped her fingers, they both thought that some changes were for the better.

***

Over the next few days, several newspapers reported missing people, but none of the cases went anywhere. There were various rumours about what people thought may have happened, but it was just gossip. No one came close to the truth. Nothing much changed in the town; people went about their business as always. At first, Zak and Wendy had decided to keep quiet about the events that they remembered for risk of no one believing them, but when Monday came, that changed. On return to school, they were sure that it would be relatively similar except for the fact that they were now the keepers of a massive shared secret, were survivors of a killer carnival, and were in the early stages of a blossoming relationship. The deep sense of warmth that they both felt for each other was the main thing that got them through the weekend without going insane. Although they had both agreed to not speak about the carnival, they had been lucky to make it twenty minutes before that went out of the window. They both had lots of questions. Neither had any answers.

They had both been correct in their assumption that no one at school had any recollection of the events that took place on Halloween. The one major thing that had changed was that their friends Kyle and Christina hadn't returned to school. Zak and Wendy hadn't seen any missing person adverts but none the less, their friends were missing. After school on that first day, they had gone to the homes of both Kyle and Christina only to be told that they hadn't returned home after Halloween. Each set of parents had made no reference to the carnival, only to Halloween. Zak and Wendy decided better not to ask anything else, then they made their way to Zak's house.

"Didn't you think that they were a little bit chilled about the whole thing?" Wendy asked Zak.

"Yeah, that was weird. You'd think if your kids went missing, you would be a mess. They seemed a little matter of fact about it all."

"Yeah, I think although the carnival is gone, some of the magic has stayed behind." Wendy shivered as she said the words. "People are acting too weird. Do you think it'll ever wear off?"

"I'm not sure. I think it's maybe just how it works. How else could it have been going all these years with no mention of it anywhere."

"Maybe we should go to the library and look through some old books. See if we can find any mention of creepy carnivals in any old true horror story or myth books. It's probably stupid, but I'm not sure what other options we have.

Zak slipped his hand into Wendy's without a second thought as they began to walk to the library. It hadn't even occurred to him how simple the transition from friends to boyfriend and girlfriend had been. They hadn't even had their first kiss yet, but he was confident that they would be together forever. He wasn't someone who believed in fate, but they had known each other their whole lives, and he knew he would do anything for her.

"Do you think Kyle and Christina are okay?" Wendy asked.

"Honestly? I don't know. I hope so, but who knows where that carnival has gone or what other types of creatures are part of it. I just hope we can find something so we can try and help them," Zak responded, feeling saddened that he didn't really believe anything they could do to help.

Just as Zak finished talking, his arm flew up, and he began pointing.

"Did you see that?" He asked, sounding shocked.

"See what?!" Wendy asked, sounding a little shocked herself at the fright Zak had given her.

"The clown...it was that clown lady. I'm positive. It was just a flash of gold ducking into that alleyway."

"Are you sure?"

"How many people do you know that wear gold and lace round about here?"

Wendy was off and running towards the alleyway instantly.

"Wait up!" Zak shouted as he gave chase. He had massive respect for Wendy's bravery, but he didn't want anything to happen to her. As they both turned into the lane — it was empty.

"Are you sure you saw her?"

"Absolutely positive."

"Oh well. I'm sure if she wants us to see her, we will."

Wendy wasn't too worried about the clown coming back to see them. She had been on their side, and they likely wouldn't have escaped without her. She was worried the clown would be punished for helping them, but she also had many questions she would like to ask her.

"Want to go to mine and read some comics?" Zak asked, still positive he seen the clown but not wanting to make a big deal out of it.

"Sure," and with that, Wendy slipped her hand into Zak's and smiled. Life would likely always be tough, but at least they had comic books and horror movies.

As they made their way through the little town, the clown woman watched them. She hopped from rooftop to rooftop, making sure no one was following them. She wasn't sure if the carnival would come back for them or not, but she had been told to look after them and look after them she would.

Five Years Later

"Zak, mate, pass me the tray over," Lee said.

"Fuck off, mate. It's your turn to roll. Get it yourself. I had to get it when it was my roll."

Lee sighed heavily and pushed himself up from the old, sweat-stained chair. He grumbled something that Zak couldn't make out and bent over to lift the lunch tray from the floor. The tray was covered in loose tobacco and cigarette papers. It had lots of pieces of torn up cardboard ready to use as roaches. Lee's fingers moved fast, even though he was heavily stoned. The papers were put together, and the tobacco filled them in seconds before he took some weed from the grinder. After sprinkling some across the tobacco, he quickly rolled it over and licked it, smoothing down the join. After rolling up a roach and slipping it into the joint, he tapped it on the table and lit it. He lay back in his chair and continued to watch the new episode of Screechers with Zak.

It was rare that Zak and Lee would do much apart from watching movies or box sets and pretty much never without also having a smoke. They rarely did anything without having a smoke. Zak had found that the only way to block out the voices in his head was to be on one type of drug or another. Anything relaxing worked for weekdays, and any upper worked for weekends. The voice or voices had become stronger over the years. The old lady from the carnival had been trying to get a message to him, and while he tried to listen at first, it all became too much. He was sure there were other voices now too, but he spent too much time fucked up to be really sure. Wendy had never heard any voices and had never seen the clown that he had seen a lot at the beginning. Their relationship had suffered, and they had each gone their own way. It hadn't been strong enough to survive. Zak had taken it badly, but he understood. She thought he was going nuts and taking drugs all the time to manage a problem that she didn't understand would have been too much for most people. The drink and drugs took the edge off the pain, but on the odd occasion he would see her, or even worse, bump into her, he still felt an intense pain in his heart. Luckily for Zak, he didn't leave his little hell hole very often.

Lee smoked the joint to the halfway point and handed it over to Zak in the ashtray. Zak took it and smoked it while he watched the show.

"It's your turn to go to the off-licence mate," Lee said.

"Aw, fuck off, I went last time."

"No, you didn't mate. Remember, I got us a pizza crunch super to half."

"Fucker. So, you did."

Zak could remember. It was the night before that he had gone. While he couldn't be fucked going, he decided better to get it out of the way and then he could chill out for the rest of the night.

"What you wanting then?" Zak asked.

"Want to just half three bottles of Buckie?" Lee offered.

"Aye, sounds good to me mate."

"Get some Highlander papers too mate."

"No hassle. Won't be long."

Zak pulled on his Nike trainers and his hoodie that had a picture of a random slasher cutting a blonde teen in half. It had got him some looks at first when he had started wearing it, but people were just used to him now. More often than not, people would be looking at him because he was stinking of weed or he hadn't had a shower, and other chemicals were sweating out of his pores.

As he closed the door to his tiny flat behind him, he realised how clean the air smelled even in the hallway. He lived on the top floor of the two up, two down. He made his way downstairs and out the front security door. It was only a five-minute walk to the off-licence, so it wasn't a major issue, but he did wish it was Lee's turn again. The breeze coming in from the sea was cold. It was always cold as it approached Halloween. He tried to stay at home as much as possible through October and November. It was pretty easy. Both Lee and he worked from home, and while they were both lazy, they always made sure they did enough work to have money for their drink and drugs. Outside of that, they didn't really give a fuck. Lee fixed laptops, computers, phones, and other bits and bobs of tech, while Zak bought old dolls from charity shops or car boot sales and turned them into horror dolls. While both could have likely made a decent living from it, neither was interested. They just needed enough to get by, and when one of them was a bit fucked, the other would cover. Their entire friendship was built on the basis that they had similar needs, and they got on okay. A bit of trust and familiarity had come from living together and being in each other's company constantly, but that was as far as it went.

Zak got to the shop mainly on autopilot as he daydreamed, pulled the heavy door open and went inside. The heat hit him instantly. It was lovely, and it brought on his stone a little more. He wandered around the aisles, looking before grabbing a packet of gummy bears and a packet of gummy hearts. He picked up a multi-pack of Cheetos and made his way to the counter.

"Three bottles of Buckfast, pal," he told the counter assistant.

The assistant quickly grabbed them and rung everything up.

"Twenty-three pounds mate."

"Oh, shit. Give me a packet of Highlander papers too."

The assistant grabbed them from the shelf below the counter. They hid all the large papers there that no one would ever use to roll a cigarette.

"Twenty-four pounds mate."

Zak handed the money over and grabbed the bag with everything he had purchased. He made his way back out of the store into the chilly October winds. As he began to walk away, he thought he heard someone shouting his name. He turned around; there was no one there. He was just about to leave and head back home to his boggin but warm flat when he noticed a flyer in the shop window. There were flyers plastered all over the inside of the window. There always had been. Some were ancient, and some newer, but it wasn't all that often people put things in these days. Most people used online for advertising or selling stuff, but a few of the towns older residents still liked to put a card in the window.

The flyer that drew Zak's attention, though, was not a sales advertisement. It was a flyer for a carnival that was coming to town — a carnival called Halloween Land. Zak almost dropped his bag.

"What the fuck. No way. That can't be real."

He moved closer to see if it was an old flyer from years ago, but when he got up next to the window, he could see it was dated October that year. Not five years ago.

"This has to be bullshit."

Zak turned on his heels and ran the rest of the way home, stopping every so often to catch his breath as he smoked far too much. He knew he couldn't tell Lee. Lee would think he was crazy. He'd never told him any of the story. He had never told anyone. He was going to have to try and get in contact with Wendy.

Wendy's House

Wendy lay on her bed, flicking through channels that had absolutely nothing on that she wanted to watch. She had gone through Netflix and Amazon Prime a load of times — nothing looked interesting. Her friends had decided to go travelling for a month, and Wendy had decided not to go. She was saving up for a car and felt that it would give her long-term freedom rather than just a holiday. It might even help her get out of this town. She kind of regretted it now, though. This was the first weekend they had been away, and she was bored out of her skull.

After deciding it was a lost cause, Wendy got up and went downstairs. She still lived with her parents, which meant that the fridge was always stocked. She grabbed some premade pancakes and syrup and quickly warmed them in the microwave. Next, she added some spray cream and plopped herself down in front of the living room TV. She put on repeats of Still Game and kicked the recliner out as she munched her food. She had seen every episode a million times, but she always liked to be watching something when she was eating — it added to the effortless comfort.

Just as she was finishing up her pancakes, the house phone rang. She never normally answered the house phone as it was never for her. All her friends called her mobile, and her parents were normally downstairs to answer it. On this occasion, as she was home alone, she decided she would answer and take a message.

"Hello," Wendy said.

"Wendy… is that you?"

The caller sounded like he was out of breath.

"Wendy, it's Zak. I need to see you. Can you come and meet me? Or I can come to you."

Wendy was surprised. She hadn't seen Zak in so long, and here he was calling her out of the blue and asking to meet her.

"Is everything okay Zak?"

"Uh, well, not really. I need to see you. We need to talk."

"Zak, it's been so long. It's late. How about you call me tomorrow, and we'll talk?"

"Wendy, I need to see you right now… Its… it's about the carnival… it's coming back."

Wendy dropped the phone. Zak's voice came out of the receiver, but it didn't register with her. It couldn't be happening. The carnival couldn't come back. It had already been to their town. They had survived it.

Later That Evening

When Wendy had come out of her daze and picked the receiver back up, Zak was still on the line. They had agreed to meet at the entrance of the old pier.

Neither had gone near the pier since Halloween, five years before. It was still derelict. Wendy was filled with trepidation as she walked towards it but was glad to see that Zak was waiting, even if he was a shadow of his former self. He looked run down, and even though he was older, she felt he looked skinnier than when they were kids. Memories of all the time they spent together in their younger days came flooding back, and it broke her heart. How people could change. Back then, she thought they would spend their lives together and that nothing could tear them apart, but life took over. After the carnival, Zak had started to become more introverted. He had started spending less time with Wendy and begun hanging out with other kids that drank and took drugs. His personality quickly changed, and he had less time for Wendy. In return, when he did spend time with her, she no longer recognised him. They were old acquaintances that no longer had anything in common apart from horrific memories of the carnival and the missing kids from their town.

Zak noticed her walking towards him. His head was generally always facing the pavement to avoid eye contact with others. Only tending to jerk his head up every so often to look around due to his paranoia of the carnival coming back. Five years later, and that fear was coming to fruition.

"Wendy, it's good to see you," Zak said, with a nervous tone to his voice.

"It's good to see you too." Wendy genuinely meant it. While seeing Zak brought a sadness of all the things that could have been, there would always be a love in her heart for him.

"Wendy, I know you think I'm crazy. You've thought I've been crazy for a while. Maybe you're right. The one thing I do know now is that the carnival is coming back. There is a flyer for it in old Mr Saleem's off-licence near my flat."

Neither said anything for a moment.

"Are you sure it's the same carnival? Couldn't it just be a coincidence?"

"It's called Halloween Land, just like last time, and it's coming to the pier again. You know the pier is in no fit state for a carnival, at least not a normal one — it has to be Halloween Land. I bet there is no sign of anyone, and then on Halloween, it'll just appear again. No one remembers it apart from us."

Wendy looked on the verge of tears. "It can't be. It just can't. We have already been through it all. Surely it's not coming back for us."

"I don't think so. If it was, I think it would have been back before now. Maybe it has some draw to the town, but I think it's just another stop on its tour of evil."

"But what can we do?" Wendy asked.

"I don't know that we can do anything to be honest. If we run all over town telling people an evil carnival is coming and that it has been here before, people will just think we are insane. Especially me."

"So, why did you call then?"

"Would you rather I hadn't, and you heard from someone else?"

Wendy sighed. "I suppose not."

Zak gave her a small smile. I'm sorry it's under these circumstances, but it is *really good* to see you again."

"You know you look like shit, right?"

Zak laughed. "Yeh, it's been a tough few years.

"So, what now?"

"Now we prepare."

"Prepare for what?" Wendy asked.

"Prepare to destroy Halloween Land, once and for all."

"Are you fucking serious?"

"What else can we do? What if it took your mother or father? What if it takes anyone you love this time? Are you okay to just hope for the best? What if it comes back again after this and just keeps coming back? We need to end it Wendy."

"You know if we go, the carnival isn't going to let us go a second time."

"This time, we will go prepared. This time, everyone from the town comes back."

The Next Morning

Zak had barely slept a wink through the night. It was a mixture of feelings about seeing Wendy again and that the evil carnival was returning. On top of that, he hadn't smoked any weed or drank anything since before he had left to go to the off-licence. It was the longest he had gone without being high or drunk in several years.

Halloween Land

After getting showered and dressed, something else that wasn't routine for some time, Zak dug out the old card from the mystic. They were some of the only things he had kept when he moved out of his parent's house. He wondered if the strange clown or mystic would be there this time. Would he and Wendy have anyone on their side on the inside?

Lee was passed out on the sofa as Zak pulled his boots on. He had arranged to meet Wendy in the old seafront café to discuss their next move.

It took Zak five minutes to walk to the café. It was a fresh morning, but Zak enjoyed being up and about — fresh for the first time in a while, he welcomed the nip in the air.

Wendy was already inside when he got there. She was sitting sipping from a cup of tea.

"Not eating?" Zak asked.

"I thought I would wait for you. Are you getting anything?"

"Definitely, I'm normally rough as a dog in the mornings. I'm getting a full English."

Zak waved the waitress over and ordered two full English breakfasts and a fresh pot of tea.

"Did you get much sleep last night? Zak asked."

"Nope. Think I nodded off a few times here and there for about ten minutes, but that was it."

Wendy poured Zak a cup of tea from the pot already on the table.

They both fell into a slightly awkward silence as they sipped at their tea. They had been apart so long, and now they were back together for the worst imaginable reason. As both of them were working on what to say next, a small tortoiseshell kitten jumped up on the table.

"That's Luna." They heard old Mrs Morrison say. She had owned the café since before either of them were born. She looked old when they were first brought in as kids, and she looked old now. Neither Zak nor Wendy had any idea what age she was, but she was always at the counter — watching over everything. Most of the staff were related to her. She could have retired a long time ago, but she seemed to enjoy being about the town folk.

"She's gorgeous," Wendy said and tried to stroke the kitten. "New addition to the family?"

Old Mrs Morrison smiled. "Some young blood to keep Carlito and Ariel on their toes.

They are too fond of sleeping, so I thought I would bring Luna in to cause some mischief."

Wendy noticed how deep Mrs Morrison's smile lines were. She was a happy old girl. Zak was right; they couldn't let an evil carnival turn up every few years and take people from their town. Who knows who it might take.

As their breakfast arrived and sat down in front of them, Kid, the café's resident Pomeranian arrived by Zak's leg.

"He's had plenty," Mrs Morrison said.

She said that to everyone, and all three cats knew better than to stand on a table when food was served. Everyone knew that if the health board ever came in, she would likely get shut down, but it was a small town, and no one like that came around. Besides, everyone liked the woman and her pets, so who would complain. As

Halloween Land

Zak and Wendy ate in silence, they sneaked the kitten and dog some slithers of bacon or small pieces of square sausage from their plates. Carlito and Ariel remained asleep on the bay window that overlooked the seafront.

Wendy broke the silence first. "So, you mentioned going prepared. You got a plan, or are we just going in there with a few kitchen knives?"

"Well, a plan is a bit of a stretch. I do have some weapons we can use, and we could take Lee for back up.

"No Lee. He's a fuck up."

"Wow, don't hold back," Zak said, smiling.

"Just you and I. We know what we are getting into. It's up to us."

"Okay, I think we should go in costume. If we go wearing slasher type costumes, it'll be easier to carry multiple weapons without looking suspicious. Also, once everyone else disappears, it'll just be us and the carnival."

"Do we even know that will happen this time? It didn't happen last time until we came out of the funhouse."

"True, we don't really know anything. It might not even look the same when we get there. I think we both know the carnival won't make it easy for us. I'm hoping we get a little inside help again, but there are no guarantees."

"So, your plan is to turn up with a pile of weapons and hope for the best?"

"I was looking at it more like turning up with a fuck load of weapons and slaughtering as many of those carnie cunts as we can before taking down the funhouse."

"Yeh, well, it does sound cooler when you say it that way, but I do feel your plan lacks a bit of substance."

Zak's heart sunk. He had hoped that for all their differences that something as important as this may have brought them closer, at least for the task at hand, but now he worried that he may have to do this on his own or with Lee — was right, he was a fuck up. Then he noticed a smile creep to the edges of her mouth.

"It's just as well you came to me. Looks like I might have to save your ass again.

At that moment, Zak saw some of the old Wendy come back. Their breakup had affected her too. She just hadn't turned to drugs and alcohol to deal with it.

"One more thing," Wendy said.

Zak nodded.

"No more drink or drugs. At least not until after we see if we make it out of this alive. I want you straight. Afterwards, you can do what you like."

Zak looked Wendy over, thoughts of what could have been flashed through his mind. It brought a lump to his throat, but he knew that was in the past now. He downed the rest of his tea and stood. He outstretched his hand and said, "deal."

Wendy shook his hand. Zak left enough money on the table to cover their tea and breakfasts.

"Come to mine later today, and we will come up with some options." Zak left knowing he had to come up with a plan, but he also had to tidy the flat and get rid of Lee so he and Wendy could talk. He couldn't go to Wendy's as he knew her parents no longer liked him.

***

The next few days were spent coming up with various ideas before both Wendy and Zak agreed they were all shit. It was practically impossible to plan for something when you had no idea what you were walking into. Zak had been stockpiling weapons though. Wendy had no idea where he had got them all and doubted that many of them were legal.

The one thing they both agreed on was the slasher costumes, so Wendy had designed them both and sown together the outfits that could accommodate their arsenal. She had added pockets and latches to conceal some of their weapons and attach other items like small plastic bottles filled with petrol. They would each have a variety of weapons that anyone could see — as that would be part of the costumes. But they wanted to carry as much on them as they could without it becoming too cumbersome. Each would also carry a holdall with extra artillery, but they both knew that at any point, they may have to drop and leave those behind. For this very reason, Zak had suggested they use up the items in the bags first and keep the items on their person for as long as possible.

The days passed quickly, even though both of them had no sleep. Wendy had pretty much stayed at Zak's round the clock, telling her parents she was staying at a girlfriend, Pamela's house.

Lee had been sent to his room by Zak and wasn't too happy, but Zak bought him a bag of weed, which seemed to sort things out between them.

By the evening before the carnival came, they were both exhausted. Zak produced two Valium from his pocket.

"Listen, I know you're against drugs, and you've seen that I am behaving myself, but none of us has slept properly for days. We need as much sleep and as much energy as possible. We need to get an early night and sleep to a decent time in the morning. We both know nothing will happen until after dark tomorrow."

Wendy just nodded. She took one of the pills and swallowed it back. Zak did the same.

"You take the bed and I'll take the couch," Zak said.

"See you in the morning," Wendy said. She walked to the door of the bedroom and looked back as Zak got settled on the couch. "Zak?"

"Yeah?"

"I'm sorry things never worked out between us."

Zak looked at her and slowly nodded solemnly. "Me too."

Halloween

When Zak and Wendy woke on the 31st of October, they both felt refreshed. It was the best nights sleep that either had had in several days. Each of them knew what was coming tonight, but there was nothing they could do about it until darkness fell. Zak couldn't remember the last time he had wanted to have a smoke so much, but he had to make do with cigarettes because he had promised Wendy there would be no more drugs. He had never considered weed to be a drug, but he knew that this wasn't the time to push it.

Unlike five years ago, when the two had been youthful and excited, they now both felt old and worn. In some ways, it felt like a lifetime had passed since that fateful day, and in others it seemed just like yesterday. Life can be funny like that.

"So, loaded question. You think either of us will make it out of this alive?" Wendy asked as she poured herself a bowl of cornflakes.

"Truthfully?"

"Yeah."

"We made it last time, but I suspect Halloween Land will know why we have come back. It may even have come back for us, so it could be tougher this time. We also don't know how to destroy the thing which could be problematic," Zak said.

"So no then?" Wendy replied.

"Well… yeah. I suppose there is a good chance of neither of us coming back, but that doesn't mean we won't win. Maybe we will destroy it, but it'll take us with it. I'm really not sure. All I know is that we don't have a choice. Could you really go on, knowing it was out there, stealing souls, and we could have done something about it?"

Wendy thought about it for a few moments before replying. "No, I suppose I couldn't live with myself."

"Trust me Wendy, you don't want to live a life filled with regret. The last five years…" then Zak trailed off.

"The last five years what?"

"Nothing. Never mind. Let's check everything one more time to make sure we haven't forgotten anything."

Later that night

The day had passed by slowly. At six o'clock Zak and Wendy had gotten into their costumes. Both were dressed as a rip-off Jason Vorhees character. As Zak looked Wendy over, he couldn't believe she still managed to look sexy in something like that. Her body had filled out over the years. Her costume clung to her hips and thighs, where she had put a strap on each leg to hold two different hunting knives. Zak had acquired quite the collection of weapons over the years, and they planned to take as many as they could comfortably. As he began slipping small knives into some of the small sown pockets where they could lay flush, he noticed her breasts were noticeably bigger too. After everything was over, Zak promised himself he'd get his life back on track — if they survived. No more speed, coke, eckies, MDMA or any of the other shit he used to distract himself from real life. If they made it, he would have achieved something worthwhile. More than worthwhile, he would have saved hundreds if not thousands of lives. That was something to think about another day if he made it through this. Right now, mission one was to end the crazy carnival for good. Job number two would be to win Wendy back.

As Wendy finished strapping weapons to herself, she came over to Zak and helped him attach a few more to the costume and hide some in the concealed parts of the suit.

"Ready?" She asked.

"I was born ready," Zak said, not sounding all that sure. He wasn't sure if he meant it as a joke or to be serious, but he was as ready as he would ever be. His mind was set on what had to be done, and nothing would change it.

"You okay?" Zak asked in return.

"Yeah... I'm glad we're going together."

"Me too. Wendy... Listen..."

"Zak, don't. Let's go to the carnival together. Anything else we can speak about afterwards, okay?

They were both silent for a few seconds, then Zak answered. "Okay. Drink for good luck?"

Wendy shook her head. "You know, this one time, I think it's a good idea."

Zak disappeared into his room and returned a minute later. "I had to hide this from Lee," he said, showing her an unopened bottle of Aberlour A'bunadh. "This is good stuff. It's strong though. We will just have one."

Zak poured two sizeable glasses of the malt whisky and handed one to Wendy.

"Just the one?" she said, looking at the glass.

"Well, you know, it's one glass. Maybe a few shots," he said and smiled.

Wendy raised her glass. "To destroying the evil piece of shit that is Halloween Land."

Zak smiled, clinked her glass and said, "I'll drink to that."

Zak slung his back in one go, and it barely registered on his face. Wendy took a sip, screwed her face up and coughed.

"Fuck sake Zak, strong enough?"

"Told you. It's good stuff. Will keep us warm and gives you that extra wee kick of bravery. I think we may need it."

Zak filled a small hip flask, slipped it into the one remaining pocket, and buttoned it closed. He left the rest of the bottle lying on the table for Lee. He hoped Lee would see it and drink the entire thing. It might prevent him from going to Halloween Land that night and may just save his life. He had no idea if the carnival would take others before him and Wendy could take it down — if they could take it down that was.

They looked each other over, ready to leave. They were both like an evil horror version of Arnie in one of those old movies where he would take out an entire army independently without being shot once.

"Let's go to the fucking carnival," Wendy said as she made her way to the door.

Halloween Land

As they approached the old pier, they could see the lights flashing. Calliope music travelled in the air marrying with the sweet and savoury smells of the carnival.

"Looks like an ordinary fucking carnival from here," Zak said.

Apart from that one statement, they were both silent on the rest of the walk down to the pier. There seemed to be no one anywhere. They had been the first ones into the carnival the last time and had arrived even earlier this time. It wasn't even supposed to open for another hour, but they had to make sure no one beat them in. It was the closest they could come to trying to make sure no one else was taken this time. They also hoped that they could sneak in before the carnival came to life. They could see all the rides and stalls were lit up, but they couldn't see any carnies anywhere. That is until a dark shadow came into sight, hopping from one roof to the next. Before they could even see the colour of her clothes, they both knew it was *the* clown. As she got closer, she dropped into the centre of the boardwalk, the lights immediately illuminated her.

She hadn't aged one day. Her beauty was breathtaking, even with the clown make-up. She still wore white and black make-up around her eyes and mouth. She was in the same weird outfit; black and red pop socks, bare legs with little wine-coloured shorts with white lace around the leg holes, black vest with a large blue silky bow around her neck. As it was five years prior, her puffed-out, long, ginger hair was topped off with a gold top hat with a blue and wine oversized bow wrapped around it and white lace cuffs around her wrists.

As she got closer to Zak and Wendy, she started waving manically with both hands, her smile wide across her face. She cartwheeled a few times, done a few backflips and then skipped the rest of the way towards them. When she came to a stop in front of them, neither knew what to say. Her eyes were both rolling in different directions. Her left eye was green and rolling clockwise, while her right was red and rolling anti-clockwise.

"Kiddywinks, hello. I must say. It's good to see all three of you."

Zak and Wendy looked at each other. The clown was clearly loopy, but from the last time they had met, they hoped she was still on their side, and they knew she could hold her own.

"Um…. We didn't expect to be back here, but we were hoping for some help from you if you were still here." Wendy said.

"Am I still here? It's hard to tell. Nothing works properly anymore."

"We can see and hear you, so you are most definitely still here," Zak responded.

"Hmmm. I suppose that's good to know. I'm not entirely sure that I wish to be still here. Isn't it a conundrum?"

"To be honest. We were hoping you would help us take this place down. Maybe you could escape with us when it's done." Wendy offered.

"You see, the mystic, Madame de Rosemonde. She is gone now. She wanted me to help you, but she has been gone for a while... I think."

"The old woman who gave you the card and told you to look after us?" Zak asked, knowing the answer but shocked to hear the news.

"Possibly. I mean probably. No, on second thought, she is. You are entirely correct. How did you know?" the clown answered.

"What? How did we know she was gone? You just told us. You aren't making a whole lot of sense," Zak said, starting to sound angry. His patience was beginning to wear thin quickly, and he had a feeling that this wasn't just a bad start, that this may be an omen of things to come.

"Yes. I believe you may be right." The clown banged the side of her head several times. "It's never been the same since I arrived. You know. The sponge in your head." Her eyes rolled even faster as she seemed to try and concentrate.

Wendy stepped closer, "Do you think you will be able to help us?"

"I will most maybely try."

"Well, that's something. I'm not convinced that's a word, but none the less, it would be good if you stuck with us."

The clown began dancing a sort of jig on the spot. It continued for a good thirty seconds before she stopped and looked them both over. "Hadn't we better get a move on then? There is no time for dancing you know."

Zak and Wendy looked at each other in amazement.

The clown began to skip away, back into Halloween Land.

"Well, at least she is here. I think that's a good thing. Right?" Wendy said.

"Fuck it. She might be crazy, but the crazy bitch helped us last time. It's all we have. Let's follow her."

As they crossed the start of the pier, it felt as if everything darkened. It was so slight that neither of them were sure, but they both had the same feeling. There were no carnies anywhere to be seen.

"Surely we won't be able to just walk straight up the middle to the funhouse."

Just as Wendy said it, everything started to shift. Their feet felt like they were firmly on the wooden pier, but everything around them looked to be shaking and becoming fuzzy. The calliope music became louder until it was almost unbearable, and then there was a pop, and everything went dark. It was completely silent. So quiet that all they could hear was their own breathing and their hearts pounding in their chest.

"Zak, you still there?" Wendy asked.

"Right next to you," he replied, making her jump.

Zak felt for her arm and slipped his hand down it into her hand. "Don't let go. Not until we can see again."

Suddenly the lights came back on. The clown was still with them, but everything else had changed.

"We travelled," was all the clown said.

Zak and Wendy looked around in wonderment. They were still at a carnival, but they were no longer on the pier. Everything around them was made of wood and looked really worn. There was sand beneath their feet, and everything had a distinct look of the Old West.

"The carnival is always changing and moving. It's taken us back in time. There are different carnies for each carnival. I think Samhain wants you to meet some of the other carnies," the clown said, sounding the most coherent she had since she found them. Zak noticed her eyes were rolling much slower, but as she finished speaking, they sped up again.

"Are we really in the Old West, or is this just a shapeshift of the carnival? How does it all work?" Zak asked.

"Only Samhain knows."

"Who the fuck is Samhain?" Wendy asked.

"I don't rightly know," the clown answered, her eyes spinning rapidly again— one now pink, the other emerald.

They had lost her. Neither of them knew what was going on, and the clown was beyond infuriating, but she was clearly trying to help as best she could.

"I guess we keep moving forward," Zak said. "Don't think we have much of a choice.

Wendy nodded while the clown stared off into space.

"Let's go then," Wendy said.

As they walked along the street of old buildings, they were on high alert. Neither Zak nor Wendy expected to make it very far without some trouble. They were both surprised that they had gone this long without being attacked. Within seconds of their arrival in the old-style wild west carnival, they heard the sound of horse riders. It wasn't long before the riders turned the corner and appeared at the other end of the small street.

Zak and Wendy had expected some weird shit, but the horseman that had ridden into the carnival town weren't just skeleton riders. Their horses were comprised of bone and loose pieces of flesh and muscle, holding the animal's structure together. It was a terrifying sight. The riders were dressed, but their faces, chest and hands showed them to be nothing more than skeletons.

"What the fuck do we do now?" Zak said.

"Well, we do have a load of weapons, but how do you kill a skeleton?" Wendy replied.

"Any ideas?" Zak said, turning towards the clown — who was no longer there. "Where did she go?"

Wendy pointed to the rooftop as the clown rolled over the top of one of the buildings.

"Is she leaving?" Zak asked.

"Who knows? She's crazy. Forget her," Wendy replied.

As the skeleton riders got closer, their horses stopped walking. Each of the figures jumped down. The dust kicked up around their feet. They looked surprisingly solid, considering they were missing pretty much all of their flesh and the majority of their muscles and organs.

"This place is fucking insane," Wendy said.

"Yeah, but we knew that before we came. How about we split up to distract them? There are three of them and two of us."

Wendy gave Zak a confident smile. "Let's take these boney motherfuckers down." And with that, she took off running. Zak sprinted in the opposite direction. The skeleton outlaws watched as they ran but never gave chase. Zak tried to watch where Wendy was going but lost track of her when she ran between two buildings. Zak was tempted to run into the saloon and look for a weapon but decided to keep running further back to see what he could use that was lying out in the open. It allowed him to keep his eyes on the skeletons — and while he knew he had weapons, he didn't have any guns. A shotgun seemed like a good way to blow a skeleton to pieces. They had split up, and one had gone after Wendy, another was climbing onto the roof, probably looking for the clown, and the last was slowly walking after Zak with a relaxed killer from a horror b-movie type of confidence. They seemed to be in no hurry. Zak only hoped they were relatively easy to kill. None of them had pulled a gun, but he knew there was a good chance they would have them. The last time he had been at Halloween Land, he had found that a lot of the carnies were pretty easy to kill, but he also had no doubt that they could end his own life pretty easily. He wondered why they weren't tougher, and the only thing he could come up with was they were as good as the carnival could do with its power. Either that or very few people put up much of a fight. As he slowed his run to a jog, he saw a test your strength machine. It stood out. It didn't look aged like the other machines. Again, this seemed strange, but now was not the time to think about it. Zak sprinted over and grabbed the extra-large mallet that was lying next to it. It weighed a tonne, but he could lift it, and it seemed like the ideal weapon to smash one of the skeletons with. He looked around again, hoping that he would see Wendy and that she was okay. She was still nowhere in sight. As he turned back to his assailant, the second skeleton came flying off the roof. He was trying to keep his eyes on the skeleton cowboy approaching him, but he noticed that the one that smashed into the ground was missing its head. The next thing Zak knew — the skeleton's head came flying through the air and smashed off the one that was almost upon him. It staggered and spun round to face the rooftop. There stood the clown; Zak had known she would be back. He was really beginning to like her. She gave him a delicate little wave and dropped onto her butt, her legs kicking back and forth over the side of the roof. The skeleton that had been coming for Zak had pulled its gun. It pulled the trigger, and a little red flag popped out with a 'Bang!!!' sign on it. Zak froze for a moment, trying to understand what had just happened. Quickly coming back to his senses, he lurched forward and swung the huge mallet with all his might. It completely obliterated the skeleton. Shards of it flew in every direction. Some hitting Zak, but they didn't pierce his clothes. Zak dropped the mallet, and the clown dropped from the roof. As they began to run towards the alleyway that Wendy had gone down, she came strolling out carrying one of the skeleton skulls in her left hand. A huge wooden post dangling from the other. "They ain't so bad." Was all she said as she chucked the skull. It came rolling towards Zak and the clown and stopped just before their feet. Zak immediately thought that Wendy had stolen the line from an old Rocky movie, but he was just happy that they were still all okay.

"Well, that seemed easier than I expected," Zak said as he watched the skeleton horses trot off into the distance. "What do you think is going on? That can't be it, surely?" he said, looking towards the clown.

Just as Zak finished speaking, everything started to heat up. The temperature suddenly rose faster than normal; literal heatwaves appeared all around them, blurring the landscape as they danced across everyone's field of vision. The next thing they knew, there was a loud pop, then the heat was gone. Their surroundings had completely changed. Everything had gone dark. The air seemed moist. As their eyes adjusted, they could see they were inside a giant cavern, with several caves leading off it. Water could be heard trickling down some of the walls. Then they heard a noise that sounded like power entering several large old machines. Lights came up, but it wasn't much. On the cave floor — which dipped down into a bowl shape — there were some different coloured bobbled lights and some poorly crafted wooden stalls. There were no rides, just a few carnies milling about that either weren't paying much attention to Zak, Wendy and the clown, or they just hadn't seen them yet.

"Is this normal, Clown? By the way, do you have a name other than Clown?"

"Just Clown. I can't remember my name from before."

The clown didn't look sad. Her eyes began to roll in opposite directions and changed to violet and ruby. Maybe she was trying to think of who she was before. Almost immediately, they stopped spinning and became clear. Both going yellow with her pupils becoming cat-like.

"We should go and see what's going on," the clown said and broke into a brisk march, swinging her arms at her sides as she made her way down towards the poorest excuse for a carnival that Zak and Wendy had ever seen. As they followed the clown down the hill, they read the stall names that were crudely painted on planks of wood, nailed above each stall. The spelling was terrible, but they could make out what each stall was. They had a *Guess Your Weight* stall, a bizarre variation of *'Hook a Duck'* except with blocks of wood instead of ducks. There was *Ring Toss, Shooting Gallery, Dart Throw, Bean Bag Toss* and a few others hidden by the taller stalls.

"Slow down a bit, clown," Wendy said as she and Zak jogged to try and catch up. Both were nervous, but the clown walked with confidence. So much so that she marched right into the centre of the little carnival. As she did, Zak and Wendy caught up and were surprised when every single carnie began running. Not towards them though — out of the carnival and towards the caves, higher up on the cave walls. The carnies from the current area that the carnival was located were all midgets. They were all dressed in black or pumpkin orange and wore shroud type clothes. Almost as if they were a strange little cult.

"Are they scared of us?" Zak asked. "Isn't it supposed to be the other way around?"

"Hmmm. I know not what the carnival thinks or wants, but we are most definitely meant to be here, most definitely, definitely most, sure to be."

"I think she's going loopy again," Wendy said.

"She's okay. Just got a few crossed wires. She hasn't let us down yet," Zak said.

"True, let's just not get too reliant on her in case she wigs out when we need her most. It's you and me. She can come if she makes it back… if any of us make it back."

Zak reached out and took Wendy's hand. He instantly felt every feeling he had ever had for her rush back; memories of all the good times flooded his head. "We'll make it. I promise."

Wendy squeezed his hand back, she smiled and it was genuine. Even in the middle of all of the madness. Zak was sure if he got out of the carnival alive that he would do everything in his power to fix things between them. Even if they could only be friends. It would have to be enough. Life was too short, and he didn't want to waste any more of it.

"Look over there," Wendy said, pointing to one of the higher cave entrances.

"Fuck. I guess it's those guys they are scared of," Zak replied.

Walking down into the cavern were four huge guys. Calling them guys might be a bit of a stretch. The must have been seven and a half foot tall and built like the largest wrestlers you have ever seen. They all wore dungarees with no shirts underneath. They could have been twins. The main thing separating them was that they were covered in large growths that seemed to be burst with some kind of plant life growing from them. The burst growths also leaked pus, and others looked ready to pop. Each of the giants had the growths in different places, covering what could be seen of their skin, but there was no doubt that under their dungarees would be just as grizzly.

"I don't want to fight those guys," Zak said. "I don't even want to touch them."

Wendy knew where he was coming from. They might even be able to pass on whatever had infected them by touch.

"We are going to have to kill them fast and try and keep our distance," Wendy said.

Just as she finished her sentence, the clown let out a massive howl.

Wendy and Zak half expected her to start turning into a werewolf. Nothing would surprise them when it came to the clown. She didn't start turning into a wolf though. She looked around the entrances and back at Zak and Wendy. "I've been to this one before. I remember. Well... I think I was here. Maybe I wasn't, but I know I was somewhere."

She stopped speaking and howled again. As soon as she finished, she began running towards the four goons who were getting closer.

Wendy looked at Zak. "Divide and conquer?"

Zak nodded and pulled off the baseball bat he had taped to his back. Wendy took a hammer in one hand and a long thick skewer in the other that her father used for the big summer barbeques. Just as they were about to fan out, while the clown headed straight down the middle, they heard more howls. They were from further away and definitely not from the clown that now seemed to have dropped to the floor and rolling head over heels towards the oncoming threat.

"What was that?" Wendy said.

"Sounds like somebody is howling back. Maybe she called someone. She said she had been here before," Zak answered.

"She says a lot of stupid stuff."

The next thing they knew, each entrance to the cave was filled with large dark shadows. As growling began to fill the cave, the four goons looked up the cave walls. Within seconds, two or three wolves came running down the side of the walls into the basin. They slowly moved forward, fangs on display, a low growl coming from their throats. They made their way towards the clown. Zak and Wendy were sure she was a goner. How could they beat the carnival if the clown couldn't even get this far? The next thing they knew, the clown pulled balloons out of her pocket, blew them up and started making a balloon animal. Wendy let out a gasp, then said, "She's crazy."

Zak felt he had to agree this time.

The clown, however, was making no balloon animal. She was, in fact, making a balloon gun. The wolves crept in behind her — when they were in formation, ready to attack, they sat down behind her and let their growls fade away.

"What the fuck?" Zak offered.

The clown, calm as can be, standing only a few feet in front of the four goons, pointed her balloon gun.

The four goons looked at each other, and the one furthest forward grunted something that neither Zak nor Wendy could make out.

"Oh well. Sweet dreams, tulip!"

The clown pulled the non-existent trigger on her balloon gun, and the front goons head exploded as if a shotgun had been put to his chin and fired. His body hung there for what seemed like a long ten seconds before collapsing to the ground. This set off carnage. The other three goons charged, as did the wolf pack. The clown had gone into a fit of hysterical laughter, dropped to her bum, legs crossed and began playing in the gore from her kill. She looked like a kid at the beach, all be it a very macabre one.

The wolves tore into the goon squad, and the goons lifted whole wolves and tore them in half. The fight was very two way. Zak and Wendy ran into the battle and began attacking the one goon. It allowed the wolves to get the other two circled — and between Zak and Wendy, they smashed the giant to pieces with the hammer and the bat, though Wendy got in plenty of stabs as well. When the giant fell in front of them, Zak went ballistic with the bat and smashed its head like a pumpkin.

"I fuckin' hate this place!" he screamed, blood dripping from his face.

As he stood covered from head to toe, Wendy pointed behind him — showing him that the wolves had dealt with the other two goons.

They both walked over to the clown as the wolves tucked into their well-deserved feast.

"Uh-Hm…" Wendy coughed at the clown.

The clown turned her head and looked over her shoulder with an innocent smile. She had more blood on her than Zak and Wendy put together.

"Aw, you guys. I knew you had it under control…. We did, didn't we?" She looked around as if she had only arrived after the battle.

"Yay!" she shouted and jumped up, hugging them both tight. On we shall go." She looked from one face to the next, like a mother checking her children were okay. Then her eyeballs looked like they were growing and shrinking rapidly. They rolled through a multitude of colours and then stopped on jet black.

"Yes, backwards and downwards. That's the plan." She began marching again and led them up to a different cave than they had come in. The wolves stayed behind. When she reached the door, she let out a howl, to which the wolves all howled back.

They had been walking through the cave for about five minutes when everything got warm again, and their eyes began to sting. Then there was a blast of light. The carnival took them to a post-apocalyptic theme park in a world that looked to have been ravaged by zombies where they had seen a zombie Kyle and Christina. The clown had been right. It was too late to save them. They were taken to an underwater carnival where they seemed to be able to breathe okay. They then found themselves at a carnival on a different planet completely, and then a carnival that they were sure was in Hell. The real Hell. The big red devil kind of hell. That had been one of the toughest ones to get through. All three of them were cut and bruised. The clown was surprisingly in the best shape. Even when she wigged out and did something so random that she should have been dead, she still managed to come through everything fine. Zak had been hurt the worse when he was attacked by a giant crab-scorpion type hybrid in Hell, but he hadn't lost any limbs. Maybe a bit of blood. Wendy had been punched square in the eye from an angry-looking mermaid or selkie or some other kind of sea creature in the underwater carnival, but she still had one non-swollen eye. Their clothes were torn, and they were running low on weapons, most having been dropped in fights or left in the bodies of their foe. They were both at the point of believing that there was no way to win, that the carnival was just going to jump them through time and space until they died of old age — if none of the psychotic assortment of carnie freaks got them first.

On the last heatwave that wasn't helping with their exhaustion, they were finally returned to the original carnival in their home-town. It looked like it, at least, and they had no reason to believe otherwise. They were positive if the carnival had chosen, it could have taken them anywhere.

"I need to sit down," Zak said, leaning back against one of the wooden stalls and sliding down it until his ass hit the floor. Wendy followed suit. The clown was away in a world of her own, mumbling something to herself and dancing on the spot. She was still covered head to toe in gore, but none of it was her own blood. She seemed to get great pleasure in playing in the blood of her enemies.

"Is this it? Have we won? Did we lose? Was there any point to what we just did at all?"

Halloween Land

Wendy asked Zak, ignoring the clown completely.

"You know better than that," Zak answered.

"What? I have no idea what you mean."

"Come on, you watch a lot of movies, or you did anyway. What always happens at the end? Big boss scene."

"Fuck off! We've killed everybody. Surely that's it. Why us? Why did this carnival pick us?"

"It didn't. It picked Kyle and Christina. It let us go. We came back for the carnival… and now… it has to kill us."

Just as Zak said it, they heard the funhouse come to life. The machines beneath it kicked in, and the lights came on. The only one who didn't immediately spin towards it was the clown.

"Here we go. The boss," Zak said.

Wendy could hear the slight smile creeping through in the way he said it. She knew that he too, would be worried about dying, but he always had to be right. It was one of the things she hated about him, even when she had loved him. Maybe it wasn't so bad. She would decide later — if they made it off the pier alive.

As the thought rushed through her mind, the exit door of the funhouse exploded open. It took a second for the dust and debris to clear enough for any of them to see who or what had come out of the funhouse. As it settled, Zak and Wendy gasped simultaneously. The figure who stood in front of them had to be at least eight foot tall. Much like the pumpkin-headed clowns that they fought the first time they came to the carnival, the figure had a live pumpkin for a head.

Wendy turned to the clown who was pulling balloons from her pocket again. "The boss?" she asked.

"The Honcho. Honcho Heady McHaunchingson. Bossiollio Numero Uno. The Dude in the Chair. First One on the Joint. Viscount Von Asshole…"

The clown kept rambling as Wendy turned to Zak.

"The fuck?"

"Ye… Well, you did say it might just be us."

While Zak and Wendy looked at each other, the clown finished blowing a long straight balloon up and sat it on her shoulder.

Her voice going super posh, she waved her other hand high in the air, "Hiiii honey!" and with that, she pulled the air trigger. What she had made this time wasn't a gun. It was a rocket launcher. The rocket found its target — the explosion was deafening. The two kids were blown off their feet, but the clown somehow was unaffected.

Zak and Wendy waited a second before they tried to get up. Both were sore and tired. Lying on the boardwalk wasn't the worst part of their day. They both leant upon their elbows then pushed up onto their feet.

"Suppose we better do this," Wendy said.

"Guess so. Hey... Wendy?"

"If we make it through this... Do you think... Maybe we could go on a date sometime? I know I fucked up, but... I really miss you."

Zak felt stupid saying it right now when they were both about to face the worst threat of their lives, but he also wondered if he didn't say it now, he maybe never would.

"How about we just focus on getting out of here alive. If all goes well, maybe you could take me for a cup of tea," Wendy said, giving Zak a reassuring smile, despite the danger they were in.

Zak smiled back and nodded. It was enough for now. "Don't they usually say something cool in the movies right about now?"

"You mean cheesy?"

"Cheesy cool."

"What you got?" Wendy asked.

"How about… When this is all over, it'll be raining pumpkins!" Zak said in his best tough-guy voice."

"Wow. That's more cheesy shit."

"What you got then?"

"Uh…"

Just as Wendy was trying to come up with something, the clown began quickly and repeatedly tapping them both on the shoulder. They turned to see where she was nodding her head. The massive freaky pumpkin-creature was standing exactly where he had been. The balloon bazooka had done nothing.

"You not got any bigger, badder balloon weapons?"

The clown took her hat off and scratched her head. She looked in her hat and shook her head no. She looked sadder than usual. Both her eyes were pumpkin orange now and bounced from side to side.

"Fuck it. I'm tired. I'm sore. I'm pissed off. Christina and Kyle are zombies. Let's just kill this cunt!"

"Not exactly cheesy cool, but yeh, fuck it. Pumpkin pie dough everyone!" Zak grinned, giving Wendy the side-eye.

"Nope."

As she answered him, she began running at the huge figure. Zak sprinted after and never looked back for the clown. As Wendy reached the monstrosity. If flicked its large black hood back, exposing even more of its orange head. It was much more life-like than the old pumpkin-heads, and it had intricate carving surrounding the sides, almost the way teens have designs shaved into their hair. Zak and Wendy didn't know it, but it was Pictish writing. The language and symbols used in Scotland when it had been called Pictland. They were said to have been a wild people — barbaric. They beat the Romans. Maybe this had been one of their gods, maybe not. No one knew very much about the Picts, but no one could deny the carnival and this creature were magic. The clown had mentioned Samhain earlier. Zak and Wendy both knew this was him.

Wendy had taken the long sharp skewer out as she ran for the freak head-on. Before she got close enough to try to stab, a long orange taloned arm swung out and back-handed her off her feet. She hit the floor of the boardwalk with a squeal.

The creature's mouth was moving as Zak got closer as if it was trying to say something, but he couldn't understand the words. It was easy enough to tell it was enraged with them, but that was all Zak knew. He pulled the two bottles out of his jacket that he had filled with petrol. He opened the tops and launched them at the freak. As they were flying through the air, he already had his Zippo lighter out and lit. He chucked that too, his aim good and the freak was shrouded in fire. It stood where it was, unmoving. Zak ran over to Wendy. She was just coming round, the fall to the ground having knocked her momentarily unconscious. He helped her to her feet and turned back to the freak. It remained stood stalk still.

"Isn't it going to die?"

"A bazooka didn't kill it." Wendy said, as she realised her jaw was now killing her.

"Yeah, but it was a balloon bazooka."

"Yeah, but you've met the clown, right? She's pretty special."

"Where the fuck is the clown?" Wendy asked.

As she asked, the clown came cartwheeling in from the side.

"You called, Miss Wendy?" the clown said.

"It's just Wendy."

Wendy kept looking over Zak's shoulder, trying to see when the pumpkin-freak was going to attack, but he still stood in the same spot.

"I set a fire," the clown said.

"Yes, you fired a bazooka, and Zak set the freak on fire. So what. He's not dying. Why isn't he attacking us?" Wendy asked. Sounding exhausted.

"The fire is burning," the clown answered.

"Arrrgghhhh. Zak. Will you talk to her?"

"Fire in the basement," the clown said.

"You set a fire? In the basement?" Zak looked round at the funhouse. "In there?" he asked.

"The clown began nodding enthusiastically. Her eyes stopped moving from side to side and settled. Her pupils returned, and her eyes both turned emerald green and stayed that colour.

"He never leaves the basement. Never! He came outside. I got in. Never trust a clown." She tried to smile, but it was still sad.

"So what, we can't kill him, but we can kill the funhouse?" Zak asked.

"The funhouse is the carnival, its heart. The pumpkin-freak as you say…. He is just a show… a magic… a…"

"You mean the freak is just a representation of what the carnival portrayed as itself?"

The clown's eyes rolled a little, then settled again. "Uh, I think so. My mind still isn't my own."

As they spoke, the freak still hadn't moved. The flames began coming out of the burst door, and then more appeared between some of the boards. The kids flopped back onto their asses. If they weren't still worried about dying, they would have probably fallen asleep where they lay.

"You think it'll work?" Zak said, looking at the clown who sat down next to him, cross-legged. She nodded. A tear ran from her eye.

"What's wrong? It's good. We won."

A tear rolled from the clown's other eye.

"Zak, leave her. I told you. She's crazy."

The clown jumped up. Gave Zak a final sad smile and jumped up, catching onto a rooftop and hoisting herself over it, and she was gone. Zak tried to get up but fell back.

"Crazy," he said to himself.

Zak and Wendy lay next to each other, still weary that the pumpkin-freak might move. But as more of the funhouse began to burn, more of the freak melted. All around them, stalls, games and rides vanished. The smell of the treats faded, and as the funhouse collapsed in on itself, it became transparent and then it was gone. As they looked out at the sea, Wendy lifted her hand and put it on top of Zak's.

"Don't forget. You owe me a tea date."

"Yeah… about that… I think things are moving too quickly."

Halloween Land

Although it hurt every muscle in her body, she rolled over and punched Zak in the shoulder. She called him an asshole as he screamed, the shock shooting through every muscle.

It was a long time before they could get up, and when they did, they kept their hands linked as they left the pier.

"I wonder what happened to the clown," Zak said.

"Oh, who cares. She was hard work."

"Yeah, but I mean, she saved our asses. I don't know that we would have made it without her. She took a risk. I think she just wanted a friend."

"Maybe," Wendy said, feeling bad. Zak was probably right. It had just been an intense situation, and she wasn't in a making friends place at the time.

"You think we will see her or the carnival again?"

"I don't think we have seen the last of either of them to be honest," Wendy replied.

The End

Halloween Land

Epilogue

Zak and Wendy sat sipping tea in Mrs Morrison's café. It had been two weeks since the carnival. Zak and Wendy were back in a position where they were the only two people in town who knew what had happened. They had met every single day for tea since the night on the pier. Neither brought it up much. They tried to talk about old times, old movies and general stuff. If they had spoken about that night and someone overheard them, they would likely have been sent away to the nuthouse.

Since they had gotten home, not much had changed except they were getting closer again and Zak's flatmate had disappeared. It wasn't strange, he had taken his stuff with him — so had obviously found someone else more fun to drink and take drugs with. Zak would have given anything to ask Wendy to move in, but he knew it was too soon. He did convince her to come back for a movie though. That made him happier than he could remember being for years.

They took their time walking home. Zak hadn't smoked a single cigarette, never mind a joint since that night. He still had a few beers at the end of the day, but he was making many steps in the right direction.

As Wendy and Zak got back to his flat, he went to put the key in the door, and it swung in. He instinctively pushed Wendy back, but she moved forward, knowing she would never let Zak investigate himself.

A little part of each of them wondered if Lee had come back. They could hear the television on as they crept in. The intruder was not trying to hide their presence. That worried Zak even more. They moved along the hall slowly, trying not to make a sound. Reaching the end,

Zak slowly peeked around the corner. Wendy had her hands on his shoulders, trying to peek over his shoulder when she felt him take a deep breath and then release a huge sigh. He stepped into the living room, opening up Wendy's field of vision. In front of them, there sat the clown. She was smiling at them both, and this time Zak and Wendy looked at each other, smiled and then dived onto the clown, smothering her with hugs. They both sat back and took her in. They had both thought she had died with the carnival. As they took her in, her head swung back and forth between them. Her eyes looked normal and stayed emerald green. They had focus, and most importantly, this time, her smile looked happy.

The End

Kevin J. Kennedy

Halloween Land Poem
By
James Matthew Buyers

Halloween Land

Amusement parks and carnivals,

The pleasure and the pain-

Infused with freaks and animals,

The calling of Samhain

Delivered goods to boys and girls,

The trick or treating fools,

Unwinding flesh in creeping curls

Not following the rules.

The clown began to pop balloons,

A sick and twisted smile,

And danced around as wild baboons

Halloween Land

Engrossed in wicked style.

The Fun House full or mirrors set

Recalled the fear of old

And couples dared to not forget

The stories others told.

Attacked by pumpkins smacked in gore,

Assailed by laughing gas,

The carnival had more in store

And no ride for a pass.

The dawning of the dead arose

As two began to dread

The scent of things nobody knows

Related to the dead.

With Zak and Wendy running round,

The Ferris Wheel of doom

Kevin J. Kennedy

Became the thunder underground

Insistent to consume.

A fire, a claw, a deathly stare,

But in the end, no frown

And Samhain went into the air

And they embraced the clown.

The carnival was lost to all

Amid the final stand

But those who lived would heed the call

And seek Halloween Land…

Halloween Land Art
By Mar Garcia

Kevin J. Kennedy

Halloween Land

Kevin J. Kennedy

Halloween Land

Kevin J. Kennedy

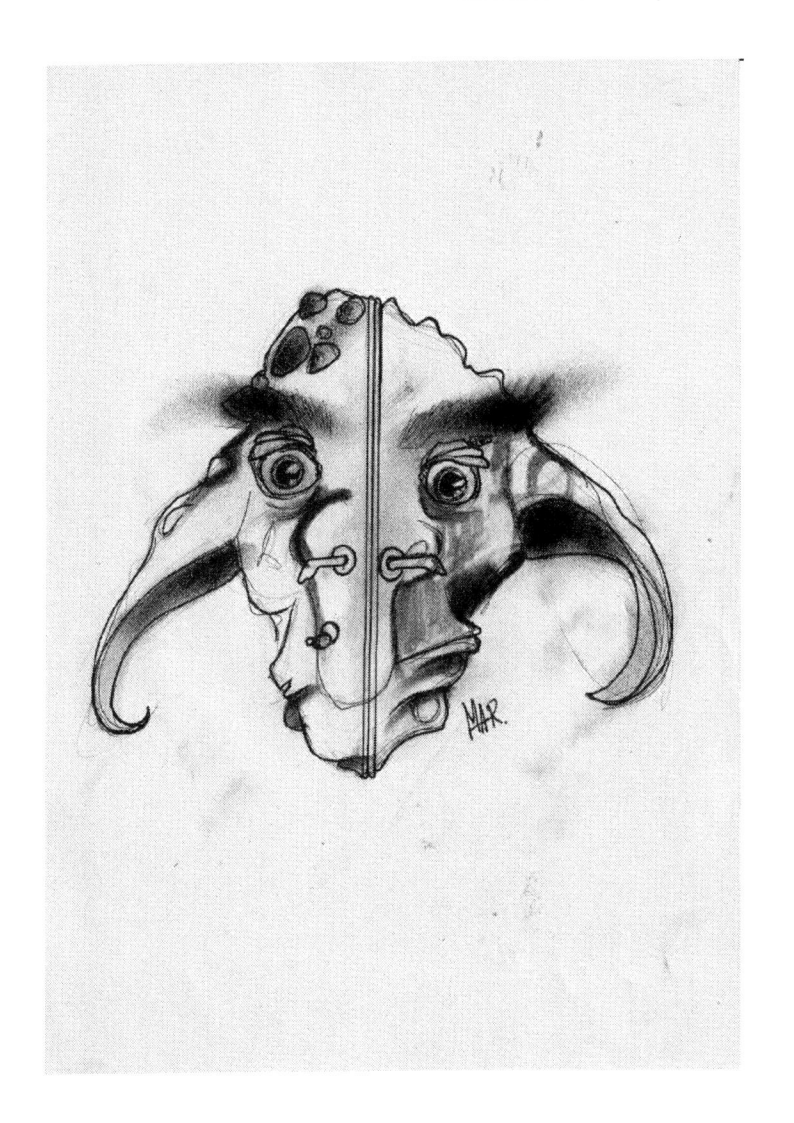

Afterword

I really hope you enjoyed my first solo novella. I love carnie horror, coming of age stories and bizarro. I felt by the end of this one it had a bit of a mix of all three. I'd love to hear your thoughts on this story, either by review or drop me a message online. I'd also love to see more Halloween Land inspired artwork. Whether you draw, paint, knit, build miniatures or any other form of art, I'd love to see what you come up with. Take a pic and tag me or send it to me. You would make my day.

Thank you once again for picking up this book. Without you, there would be no point in writing.

Printed in Great Britain
by Amazon